SHE'S DIFFERENT FROM THE OTHER ONES 3

DEEANN

Contains explicit languages and adult themes

suitable for ages 16+

TEXT UCP TO 22828 TO SUBSCRIBE TO OUR MAILING LIST
If you would like to join our team, submit the first 3-4 chapters of
your completed manuscript to

ACKNOWLEDGMENTS

First off, I would like to thank God! Without Him, I am nothing. I'm so thankful for this gift He has given me and I pray He continues to work in me.

Thank you to my husband for supporting and believing in me. The hand massages after a long day of writing mean so much; it's just the small things. I love you, baby.

To my son, everything I do is for you. You keep me going and I go harder every day to make sure you will always be straight. I love you so much and I promise I will make you proud.

Mommy, thank you for being my number one fan and always supporting me. I know I can always count on you.

UCP, we are on the rise! You all are great and I appreciate you all.

Jahquel, thank you for believing in me and being such an inspiration not only to me, but to others as well. You're an amazing mentor and publisher. You're stuck with me forever!

Brii, thank you for being such an amazing friend! You've helped me so much with my books. The feedback, the test reads, the motivating; I couldn't have done it without you. I love you!

Keish, thank you for all the encouraging words and being such a great friend! I appreciate you more than you know!

Readers, thank you for taking a chance and continuously rocking with me! You guys are the bomb!

ABOUT THE AUTHOR

Let's Chat!
Facebook: Dee Ann, Like page: DeeAnn, Reading group: DeeAnn,
What We Reading?
Twitter: AuthorDeeAnn_
Instagram: Authoress_DeeAnn
Email: authoressdeeann@yahoo.com
Website: http://deliciad23.wixsite.com/mysite

For Kita and Dj... sissy loves y'all.

1

AMARI "MARI" WHITE

"*N*o! What in the fuck just happened?" I screamed as the sound of the beeping monitor filled my ears. My head was spinning, and I felt my entire world come crashing down. Why was this happening?

"I need you all to leave," Frankie stated calmly, but I wasn't trying to hear that shit. I was staying put until they revived my brother.

"I'm not going anywhere until someone explains to me what just happened! How was he just okay and now, he's flatlined? Bring my brother back!"

I knew I sounded dramatic, but I couldn't help it. It went from me being joyful, hearing that there was a chance Ken would wake up soon, to him having a seizure and flatlining. Just when I was so close to having my best friend back, God decided He wanted him. *I'm sorry, Lord, but I need him a little more.*

My father walked over to me while my mama and Marissa ran out the room, sobbing loudly. I bit my lip and rocked from side to side as I tried to refrain from breaking down. Daddy put his hands on my shoulders and made me look him in the eyes. For the first time in my life, I saw fear. Fear that his one and only son wasn't going to be so lucky this time. He was scared, but he was trying to be strong for me, so I had to be strong for him.

"Daddy, I'm staying in here until they revive him. I... I can't leave without knowing he's okay," I cried as I looked over his shoulder at them working on Ken. My knees buckled and daddy caught me as I watched his body erupt into another seizure. I let out a gut-wrenching cry and fell into Daddy. He picked me up and carried me out the room, and someone shut the door behind him. Mama and Marissa ran over to us as Daddy carefully placed me on my feet. I just laid on his shoulder with my eyes closed and cried; I couldn't do anything else.

"What's going on, Julian? Why is she breaking down like this?" Mama interrogated in panic. She grabbed my arm and pulled me into her. She was holding onto me for dear life and I could feel her body trembling. I rubbed my hand up and down her back to calm her. This was taking a toll on everyone.

"He had another seizure," Daddy sighed, and Mama gasped. I peeked over at Marissa, who looked as if she was about to pass out. I reached over for her hand and she grabbed mine tightly; her hands were shaking too.

"How did this happen? Everything was just fine," Marissa said what we all had been thinking.

"I'm not sure, baby, but we just have to pray. Him having another seizure means he was breathing again, so we have to pray it stays that way and things get better," Daddy replied, and Mama agreed.

This had become a routine. We would all gather around Ken two to three times a day and pray. I locked hands with everyone, but in the back of my mind, I was wondering if God was even listening anymore? Day in and day out, we were praying and now look. Ken was basically dead. What if they couldn't revive him? All that praying would be for nothing.

Daddy finished and everyone recited 'Amen' except for me. I guess you could say I was in my feelings, but I was tired. I wasn't sure anymore, so I walked away to give myself some time to think and process everything. I needed Roman more than air right now, but I didn't want to bother him. He said he would text me once he was done, and I still haven't heard from him. Maybe I should call.

Out the corner of my eye, I could see Daddy swaggerin' toward me. I didn't feel like being bothered, but I knew I had no choice. Even if I chose to ignore him, he would somehow still get his point across. I had a feeling he was about to question me about the ending of the prayer, so I sat up to prepare for his lecture.

"Are you okay, Mari?" he softly asked as he sat down next to me. Like a magnet, my head went straight to his shoulder. There was something about laying on him that brought me comfort. It had been like this for as long as I can remember.

"I don't know, to be honest. I just feel numb right now."

"No, what you feel is doubt. You're doubting God when you should be trusting him now more than ever. The doctors are in there trying to bring your brother back to life and *now,* you want to give up hope? That's not the way to do things, baby girl. Never lose that faith."

He was right, but it wasn't what I wanted to hear at the moment. I wanted to have my moment. But, when I thought about it, if I gave up on my faith, then I was giving up on Ken and that wasn't my intention. I would never do that. Closing my eyes, I silently repented and asked God to bring Ken back to us.

"I'm just so scared, Daddy," I confessed, barely above a whisper. I inhaled a deep, shaky breath, then exhaled slowly.

"I am too, baby. I am too."

We sat there in silence, both consumed in our own thoughts. I pulled my phone out and sent Roman a text asking him to call me when he could. If he didn't text back soon, I was going to call. It had been a few hours since we last talked, and I was sure they were done by now. Then again, anything could have happened.

Frankie came out the room and I stood up. I watched as Marissa ran to him and embraced him tightly. He discreetly kissed her forehead, but it was obvious to me. She pulled back and our eyes met. I raised my brow at her and she shook her head no. She was lying. I know what I saw, but now wasn't the time to question it. It would be brought up later, for sure. Daddy and I walked over and waited for Frankie to say something. My mouth was dry and I was hot. The anticipation was killing me.

"We were successful at reviving Kendrick. I think his brain became too overwhelmed. He's stable," Frankie revealed, and we all breathed a sigh of relief.

"Did it make things worse?" Mama asked.

"It may take him longer to wake up now."

"As expected," Daddy mumbled while rubbing his chin.

"I say everyone goes home to get some rest. Visiting hours are almost over and it's been a long day. I promise we will keep a close eye on him tonight," he suggested, and we all agreed. I wasn't worried because Ken was truly in good hands with Frankie and the staff. They had been on top of things since day one.

I hugged everyone and headed to my car. I pulled out my phone to call Roman when I dropped it. When I bent down to pick it up, I could see that Marissa had stayed behind to talk to Frankie. The way they were just standing so close to one another comfortably pissed me off. I wanted to confront her, but I would wait for another time. I was too tired mentally and physically to be beating some ass tonight. Everyone knew I didn't play about Ken. Her ass better not be on some sneaky shit because I peeped game at her grand opening too. They were very flirtatious, but I didn't worry too much because Roman had my attention. It was time for me to speak my piece.

I made it onto the elevator just in time with my parents. We were all silent until we made it to our cars. I didn't want to go home to an empty house, so I was going to call up Jersey to stay with her and Jo. I didn't want to be alone right now.

"Be careful, baby. Try to get some rest, okay?" Mama insisted as she kissed my cheek. "Don't be up all night thinking."

"It's going to be hard not to, but I'll try," I promised.

Daddy opened my door, kissed my forehead, and I laid my head on his shoulder.

"If it becomes too much for you, call me and I'll come get you. I doubt I'll be asleep tonight. I have to make sure your mama is okay," he whispered.

"Okay, Daddy. Thank you."

"You're welcome, baby girl. I love you. Let me or your mama know when you make it home."

"I love you too."

Daddy watched me until I turned the corner. I hit the Bluetooth and dialed Roman. It went straight to voicemail. I tried three more times and it did the same. Damnit. What was he doing? With everything going on, the worst possible scenarios bombarded my brain. I shook them off and dialed Jersey. Voicemail. I was growing pissed. Why was it that the two people I needed the most wasn't answering for me? Giving up, I just went to Roman's, showered, and climbed deep under his covers. It took a while, but sleep finally consumed me.

SINCERE "SIN" PETERS

I ran out the house right behind Roman with Red's phone still in my hand. I couldn't believe all this shit was happening. How did we miss this? I can admit, since Jersey and I stopped talking, I hadn't been on my Ps and Qs like normal. I should have found Tameika the day Jersey told me what went down. My feelings got the best of me and I let my guard down. Now, my son's life was in jeopardy, and I wasn't stopping until I found him.

Roman was already in the driver's seat waiting for me. He sped all the way to our jet as I prayed that we would find them safe and sound. It seemed like Jersey and I couldn't catch a break. It had been like that since I first met her. Maybe all this shit was a sign.

"You think they're still in Birmingham?" Roman quizzed as we were pulling up to the landing strip.

"I hope so. Call up the crew and have them all searching the streets. No one does anything else until we find them."

"How we gon' do that when we don't even know what the bitch looks like?"

I didn't answer as I continued to scroll through Red's phone. I stumbled upon what I was looking for and looked over it before giving Roman the phone with a smirk on my face. That was one thing

I had to give to Red; he was very organized. With a few strokes of my thumb, I found where he kept his online files of everyone he done business with. Tameika's file was the first to pop up. Ro studied the file while I instructed our pilot to take us back home.

"Damn. So, her ass been up under our noses this whole fuckin' time? Red a foul ass nigga for helpin' her out behind your back like that."

Apparently, not only did Red give someone else the assignment, but he had also been giving Tameika information about our whereabouts. He had sold me out for ten mill. Bitch ass nigga. I knew something had been up with him lately. The way he had been moving wasn't like him. Too bad he couldn't enjoy that little bribe money from the grave. I would be getting one of the tech guys to wire it all to my account and would give Ro half, keeping the rest for myself for the heartache and suffering I endured due to my boss. I hope his ass rots in hell seated right next to the devil.

"I wish I could bring his ass back to life and do the shit all over," I fumed and sat down.

"It's over and done with now. He got what he deserved. We need to focus on getting Jersey and Josiah back."

"Agree."

The flight back was a quiet one. Ro was laid out asleep while I had hooked Red's phone up to my laptop and downloaded Tameika's file onto it. It had everything I needed to know, from her time of birth to when she got released from the pen. I clicked on a newspaper article that stood out to me. It was dated almost five years ago and I knew exactly what it was; an obituary for Tameika's "baby". There were pictures of the small funeral and everything. This was some crazy, Lifetime movie shit. How did I end up in the middle of all this?

There was also an article on the shooting, along with an obituary for Jersey's ex. By the time I was done reading over her file's contents, we were landing in Birmingham. I shut down my laptop and woke Ro up.

"Ro, wake up. We're landing."

"Already? I just closed my eyes." He yawned while rubbing his face. "What's the move?"

"We're about to go get my son, nigga."

"No plan? Just running up in that bitch?"

"Yeah." I shrugged. "If your ass didn't fall asleep, then maybe we could have come up with something."

"A nigga was tired," he chuckled with a shrug. "Nah, Sin. You ain't thinking clear, man," he expressed while tapping his head with two fingers. "We can't just run up in there not knowing what the hell we're facing. You see that bitch is crazy! Never underestimate your opponent. You know that."

I wasn't trying to hear all that think rationally shit he was trying to throw at me, but he was right. If we went in there without staking out for a few hours, then anything could go wrong. Either Jersey and Jo could be killed, us, or both, and I couldn't risk that. This had to be successful the first go 'round so we could get them out of there safely.

"So, what you got in mind?"

"Do you have a location on them?"

"Yeah."

"Aight, we need to watch the place for a few hours and see what kind of moves she's making. I doubt she came here by herself. She needed some help," he noted, and I agreed.

"Let's get to it."

We hopped in Ro's truck and listened to the GPS. The closer we got, the more my trigger finger was itchin'. I wanted to get this bitch so bad that I could taste it. Josiah was the main thing on my mind. My little man better be okay; not one scratch. This situation made me think more about adopting him. Blood couldn't make us closer, and I wanted him to have that security of knowing he would always be straight. Regardless, he would be, but doing it legally would be even better. Josiah Peters; that had a ring to it.

Ro flipped the lights and cruised down the street. We pulled a few houses down from where the GPS said they were. Ro cut the engine and leaned up. I reached in the back to grab some binoculars when my phone started ringing. It was Kacey. I thought about just ignoring her, but I wasn't trying to have us in a bad space.

"What's up, beautiful."

"Hey, Sin." She giggled. "How's everything going? I haven't heard much from you today."

I sighed loudly and rubbed my hand across my face. "I'm sorry, Kacey. So much shit has happened that I haven't been paying attention to my phone."

"Oh, you don't have to apologize. Is everything okay?" she asked with concern, which caused me to smile a little. It felt good knowing she cared.

"Not really, but it's nothing for you to worry about. What's up with you? What have you been doing all day?" I changed the subject and leaned back in my seat. I didn't feel like explaining the situation right now. My head was spinning, and I was just ready for it to be over.

"Studying. I have a big test coming up and I want to make sure I'm prepared."

"Don't stress it, baby girl. You're going to ace that shit like you always do."

"I hope so," she sighed.

"Someone's coming out the house," Roman announced and took the binoculars from me. I squinted to see what he was talking about. It was a male, but since it was dark, I couldn't make out his face. He got in the car, but never started it up. I glanced at Ro and he nodded his head.

"Hello? Sincere?" Kacey's soft voice reminded me she was on the phone.

"Yeah, my bad."

"You need to call me back?"

"Yeah, I'll call you in the morning."

"Okay. Goodnight, and be safe."

"Always. Goodnight, Kac. Sweet dreams."

I powered my phone off and placed it in the glove compartment. Checking the chamber on my .45 to make sure it was fully loaded, I set it in my lap and took the binoculars from Ro. I tried to zoom in as much as I could to get a visual, but it was too dark. Fuck it.

I got out the truck with Roman right behind me. I jogged to the car dude was sitting in and tapped on the window before breaking it, sending all the glass flying on him. Opening the door, I pulled him out and put my piece to his head. He was quivering in fear, but that didn't move me. All I cared about was finding Jersey and Jo. I bent down so I was eye level with him so I could get a good look at him.

"What's your name?" Ro asked with his gun pointed at the dude's balls. His crazy ass.

"Junie."

"Where are they?" I asked, getting straight to the point. This wasn't no damn meet and greet.

"Who?"

"The woman and the boy! Where are they?"

"Dawg, I don't know what you talkin' about. I'm not no fuckin' kidnapper!" Junie barked with a mug on his face.

PEW!

"Agh, fuck!" Junie screamed out. I looked behind me to see that Ro had shot him in the foot.

"That was a warning shot, nigga! Now, where in the fuck are they? We don't have time for you to be playin'," Roman spat and began to pace back and forth. I shrugged and turned my attention back to Junie while pressing my gun in his side. He was cursing under his breath and squirming from the pain. No sympathy.

"Now, I'm going to ask you one more time; where are they?" I demanded through gritted teeth. My temperature was rising and sweat was dripping from my forehead. I took my gun and shoved it against his temple, then cocked it. I wasn't for the bullshit anymore. "Where. Are. They?"

"I swear, I don't know what you're talkin' about, dawg. This my grandma house. I been sittin' out here waitin' on my ole lady to pull up with my daughter. She ain't allowed in my grandma house, so I was waitin' outside for her. I don't know what y'all talkin' about. I swear," he explained with a clenched jaw while looking me straight in the eyes. He wasn't lyin'. He had no clue what we were getting at. Keeping the gun on him, I pulled out my phone and checked the location I was sent. I was at the right place, so what was going on?

"Do you know Tameika White?"

He shook his head no. "Never heard of her."

"So, you've never seen this woman?" Roman interrogated while shoving Red's phone in Junie's face. Junie studied the picture and shook his head no again.

"Nah. Don't know her." A car pulled up and I trained my gun at it. "Chill! That's my girl."

Sure enough, a woman got out with a terrified expression. She slowly walked over and when she noticed Junie on the ground bleeding, she ran over and tried to pull him away. Little mama had heart. Most bitches would have stayed their asses in the car and yelled out the window. She was trying to save her man, and I respected that. I stood up and wanted to fire off some rounds in frustration. I don't understand what happened. Nah, I do. Tameika was smarter than I thought.

I started searching the car Junie was sitting in until I found what I was looking for; a tracking device. "This your car?"

"It is now," Junie answered as his girl helped him up.

"Now?" Roman repeated.

"Yeah. I bought it from some dude maybe five hours ago. He said his girl didn't want it anymore," he explained, then winced in pain. His girl was standing there grillin' the fuck out of Ro and me. She reminded me of Amari's feisty ass. I could see her bustin' a nigga for Roman.

"What's his name?"

"Vic."

"No last name?"

"Nah, that's all he told me."

Reaching in my back pocket, I peeled off a few bands and handed it to him. His girl snatched it from me and counted it. I guess she was satisfied because she smiled and put it in Junie's pocket.

"Sorry about all this shit, bruh. Go to UAB hospital and ask for

Frankie. Tell him Sin sent you and to send the bill to me. I'll have someone come out here and fix your car for you. Take that money and do something nice for your girl and daughter. Good lookin' out," I explained as I tucked my gun in my pants, then started jogging back to the truck.

My eyes started stinging, so I repeatedly blinked to make it go away, but that only made the tears fall. Rage took over and I started swinging at the air. We were back at square muthafuckin' one and I didn't know what to do. I felt hopeless, but giving up wasn't an option. I was going to find them, even if it killed me.

Roman came over and pulled me into a brotherly hug. "We gon' find them, Sin. This bitch can't keep runnin'."

"I just feel like I'm failin' Jo. This should have never happened."

"The only way you can fail him is if you give up, bruh. I know how you do, and that's not you. You're not in this alone, either. I already got word out to be lookin' for a new, young cat named Vic, and I already sent his name to the tech crew. They're searchin' for a new location also. We got the whole army out here, Sin. They can't dodge that."

"I appreciate that shit, Ro. All this shit was built up in me, but I'm good now," I explained while taking my hair down and putting it back up. The sweat had it sticking to my face and that shit was annoying. "You can take me back to my car and head home to get some sleep. I'm going to Jersey's house to see if I can find anything there."

"I doubt I get any sleep," he sighed. "I'll go break the news to Amari, then come help you. I can't let you be out here by yourself."

"I'll be good. Sis gon' need you more than I am. I'll go scoop up Tate and have him ride with me. Just hit me up later."

"Bet."

He took me back to my car and told me to call if he found out anything, and vice versa. I called Tate and he said he would be waiting for me. I took a few deep breaths before lighting a joint, then starting my car. Jo's school picture caught my eye and I couldn't help but smile while gazing at it. It did something to my heart. *Let me go find my son.*

JERSEY LOVE

"Sss, ouch," I whined as I opened my eyes and observed the dimly lit room. I was in a basement, tied to a bed, but I was lying on the floor. My ears were ringing and there was a throbbing pain in the back of my head. I could taste blood tickling the back of my throat, and I wanted to puke.

Where was Josiah? I wanted to panic, but I didn't dare want to make a noise. I was afraid that if I did one wrong thing, Tameika would kill me or hurt Jo. I had to get us out of here, but how? I couldn't call or yell for help or try to escape. I had to think of something for the sake of Jo. If I didn't make it out alive, I could guarantee that he would, and I put that on my life.

I couldn't believe that Tameika had caught me slipping. It was my fault because I forgot to set the alarm before Jo and I went to bed. I was so in my feelings about Sincere leaving that I forgot all about it. Now, here I was, paying for it. I prayed she wasn't harming Josiah or I would find a way to break free and kill that bitch. He was *my* son!

A door creaked upstairs, so I closed my eyes and acted as if I was still knocked out. Through the slits of my eyelids, I could see Tameika slowly walking down the steps with a sinister grin on her face and a huge pot. I figured it had to be full of water and I hoped it was cold and not hot. She stood over me and I tried to control my breathing as I anticipated what she was about to do next. I felt the freezing water shock my body, then a kick to my abdomen made me hover over in pain. I coughed up some blood and glared up at her.

"Rise and shine, bitch," she spat with laughter in her tone. "You can't sleep forever."

"Where is Josiah?" I asked, coughing up more blood.

"You mean, Liam? He's upstairs watching TV."

"His name is Josiah!"

"No, his name is Liam! That's what I named him before you took him away from me," she screamed and kicked me in the stomach again, then threw the pot at me. The pain was excruciating, but there wasn't anything I could do but take it. *God, please, get Josiah out of here safely. Spare my baby.*

"I saw you that night! You thought I was asleep, but I wasn't. Whatever that bitch put in my IV paralyzed me for a short time instead of putting me to sleep! I couldn't do anything but sit there and watch you take my baby!"

"Just like you took Lee away from me! Let's not point fingers when *you're* the one who started all this bullshit!" I yelled back in anger. I swear if I wasn't tied up, I would be on her ass like white on rice.

"You should have been doing your job as a woman," she stated nonchalantly with a shrug while pacing the floor in front of me. "Lee came onto me, and like any other woman, I took the bait. He would tell me every single detail of your relationship and what you weren't doing for him. So, I did it for you. You win some, you lose some."

I couldn't believe the words that were coming out her dick suckers. Never did I know the extent of their relationship, and I didn't want to know. Just knowing that Lee was cheating period was all I cared to know. To know he was pillow talking about our private life together made the heartache resurface. I tried my best to be the woman he wanted and deserved; guess my all wasn't good enough.

"Just like I'm taking care of *my* son; for you, of course," I shot back with a smirk tugging at my lips. "You know, since you weren't capable, jail bird. Was Lee really worth the years you've missed? I mean, it's not like you would be in Josiah's life anyway, but you wouldn't have missed out on your own. All for what? Some dick? No man is worth my life."

"He is when he's the father of your child. I forgot, you wouldn't know since you can't conceive like a normal woman," she taunted and kneeled down in front of me so we were eye level. "You're nothing but a pathetic excuse for a woman. What woman can't give her man the child he so desperately wants? You. That's why Lee ventured off and found a *real* woman. Did I mention Liam has a sister?" Tameika exclaimed with a devious grin. "I guess that was one thing that was left out the equation, huh?"

"A sister? How? Where?"

How could this be? Did Lee sit back and have a family on me? I knew he was fucked up over me not producing enough eggs, but he would always say there was a chance. Apparently not since he was out there giving his seeds to Tameika! Two babies? Well, at least I had one of them. That still didn't change the sorrow I was feeling. Josiah was mine, but not biologically. Once upon a time, Lee was the love of my life, and to hear that their affair went deep was damn near unbearable.

Knowing that he blamed me for him stepping out bothered me. Honestly, I never thought that was the reason why. I thought he was just out here making selfish decisions and had fallen out of love with me. I knew for a fact part of that was true. He made a selfish decision. He should have been a man and just expressed his feelings to me instead of confiding in another woman. My own damn cousin at that! Now, it had me second guessing myself and if I truly wanted to work things out with Sincere — if I got out of here.

"She's upstairs with him. Her name is Kyleigh, but we call her Leigh for short. She's two years older than him, if that tells you something. That's how long I was riding Lee's dick behind your back, bitch!"

Her little name calling didn't bother me, but her words before that caught my attention. What did she mean *we*? Who else was here and around Josiah? That explained the deep voice I didn't recognize.

"And as you can see, he never left me. Isn't that why you killed him?" I chuckled while shaking my head at her. That got under her skin. She punched me dead in the nose, then spat on me. Blood poured from my nose, and I swear I was seeing stars. I just laid my head down and closed my eyes while trying not to think about the pain.

"And as you can see, he started a family with me! Something you will *never* be capable of. You had to steal my child to make yourself feel better, right? Well, guess what? He's home with his mama now. The one who carried him in her womb for ten months and went through sixteen hours of labor! Me!" she shouted with tears staining her cheeks. "He belongs to me, so you can kiss him goodbye and be thankful for the memories — while you have them. Bitch."

WHAP!

~&~

I woke up to nothing but darkness. I couldn't see anything except for the little light from underneath the door. My head felt like it would explode from the throbbing, aching pain beating on the side. My stomach was sore, and it was a painful to breathe. I could feel my right eye starting to swell, and I could still taste the blood in my mouth. I was in desperate need of some food or water. Something.

Everything Tameika had said earlier crossed my mind. Was she being serious about Josiah having a sister? I knew there wasn't anything I could do about any of it because the past was over and Lee was dead, but that didn't change the hurt and betrayal I felt from both of them; mainly Lee. All the feelings I had buried deep inside were starting to resurface, and the saltiness of my tears burned the open wound on my cheek. I had to let it out. It had been built up for too long, and the release was welcoming.

Not only was I crying from the situation and secrets revealed, but also for Sincere. I missed him something serious, and I was so pissed at myself for pushing him away. He had been nothing but good to Jo and me; despite his lifestyle. Like he told me before, his way of living didn't define the person he was, and I knew it all along. Honestly, one of the reasons I did push him away was because I didn't think he would accept my past. I heard him saying it, but my insecurities wouldn't allow me to believe him. Now, I was regretting it, but I couldn't shake the feeling that maybe we weren't meant to be.

The light from the door turned off, leaving it pitch black. Not even the moon was shining through the small window. The window! That's how Jo and I could get out of here. Now, I just had to figure out how to free myself and get Jo from upstairs. Using a technique I saw on a movie, I started moving my hands up and down to wear out the rope that was holding me hostage. It may take a while, but I was willing to do anything to get Josiah to safety.

A few minutes later, I heard some footsteps above me that stopped at the door. They weren't too hard, but enough that I could hear them. I immediately stopped moving and played sleep once I heard the door open. My heart felt like it would beat through my chest as I heard the door open and footsteps coming down the stairs. I don't think my body could take any more of Tameika's abuse.

"Mommy?" Josiah's little voice was like music to my ears. I let out a sigh of relief and cried. I was so overwhelmed. "Mommy?"

"Jo, baby. I'm over here. Can you see me?"

"No ma'am. It dark in here and I scared," he whimpered. "I wanna go home."

"I know, baby. I know. Listen, I need you to help mommy so we can get out of here and go home, okay?"

"Sin come get us?"

"I... I don't know, but we have to hurry."

I started thinking of things I saw earlier that could help us. It would be a hard task since Jo was so young, but my baby was smart and he could help me. I shut my eyes tightly and envisioned the basement in light.

"Okay, Jo. I need you to listen to mommy. Can you try to come find me? Follow my voice," I instructed. I could hear his feet shuffling across the concrete. A few seconds later, he touched my face then wrapped his little arms around my body. It felt so good to feel his touch.

"Mommy, why do that woman call me Wiam (Liam)? I Josiah," he asked as he laid his head down on me. "And she's not my mommy, but she keeps telling me to call her that."

Stupid bitch. She had some nerve. Now, instead of fear, I saw rage. Red everywhere. I don't give a fuck who pushed him out their pussy; Josiah was MY son! I'd raised him from day one, so for her to even think of herself as a mother to him was beyond me. Yup, I stole him, which makes him *mine*! Call me crazy, but it is what it is. She considered Lee hers, right? Exactly.

"Has she been mean to you?"

"No ma'am. They been nice."

"Who is they?"

"Weigh (Leigh) and the man the woman told me to call daddy," he said, only enraging me more. I had to take a few deep breaths as I started working to tear through the rope. This was a conversation for later. The focus now was to get us out of here.

"I need you to listen carefully and do what mommy says, okay?"

"Okay."

"Feel your way over until you feel some wood. Remember what that feels like? Like the table at home?"

"Uh huh."

"Remember what a flashlight is? Like the Batman one your granny got you for your birthday?" I reminded him. Josiah had a great memory, so I knew he would remember.

"Uh huh!" he exclaimed excitedly. "The one with the pictures?"

"Shh," I hushed him not to be so loud. "Yes, baby. That's it. When you get to the wood thing, feel around for a flashlight and turn it on."

I held my breath as I listened to him scuffle around, trying to find it. I vividly remember seeing one laying there earlier. While Tameika was going on her little rant, I was doing the best I could to study the basement for things to help us escape. I was thankful I did.

"Here it is!"

"Shhh, Jo! Turn it on and find me." He did as he was told and shined the light directly in my eyes. "Come here. You see these things tied around my arms and my legs?"

He nodded his head yes with tears in his eyes. "Mommy, what happened to you face? She do that?"

"I'm okay, baby." I shrugged it off as I fought back tears. I hated that he was being exposed to a situation like this so early on. I knew it was my fault for not being careful and never thinking the past would catch up to me. It was my job to protect him, and I wasn't doing too good of a job at it. I silently promised him I would do better once we escaped. "You see these?" I reminded him of the ropes.

"Yes," he mumbled with his lip poked out.

"I need you to untie them for mommy. Remember how Sin taught you how to tie and untie your shoes?" The mention of Sin's name made him light up and nod his head yes eagerly. "That's what I need you to do so mommy can get free and give you a big hug."

"This big?" he asked while sitting the flashlight down and stretching his arms wide, and I smiled.

"As big as you want."

His little hands went to work, trying to let me free. I knew it would be a challenge for him with the rope being so rough and thick, but he was able to get it loose in a matter of minutes. I wiggled my hands to finish it off and sat up, immediately becoming dizzy and nauseous. I counted to ten and took deep breaths until it all subsided. Leaning down, I untied my ankles, then embraced Josiah in a tight, bear hug while planting kisses all over his little sweet face. Rising to my feet and ignoring all the pain shooting throughout my body, I grabbed Jo's hand and looked around with the flashlight.

Placing Josiah on the bed, I stood on it and reached for the window. With what little strength I had, I managed to get it open and welcomed the cool, refreshing night breeze. I climbed up and looked out to make sure we would be able to fit through.

"Okay, Jo. I'm going to pick you up, and I need you to climb through the window. Once you get outside, move over and wait for me. Okay?" I explained, and he nodded his head in understanding.

I kissed his forehead and picked him up when I heard movement above us. For a second, I froze, but when I heard hard, heavy footsteps coming our way, I started moving. I damn near threw Jo out the window and closed it behind him. Jumping down, I searched for something I could use as a weapon and turned the flashlight off just as the door opened. Quietly, I tiptoed behind the stairs and waited for them to come down. My body shook nervously as the creaking stopped and their feet hit the pavement.

I watched as the silhouette of a man flicked on the lights and looked to the bed where I was supposed to be. My breathing quickened as he rubbed his chin and began looking around the basement. Making sure to stay out of sight, I took in his appearance, remembering every detail that I could. He was a big, stocky guy and for a second, I feared what would happen if he found me. Then, I remembered Josiah was outside waiting for me and sucked it up. He was going to find me regardless, so I decided to act first.

I waited until his back was turned when I stepped out and knocked him over the head repeatedly with an old, rusty baseball bat. His body fell to the ground with a loud thud, but I still continued beating him. I wanted to make sure he would be out until someone came and found him. Leaning down, I made sure he was still breathing, then searched his pockets for a phone or something. I came across his wallet and decided to take it with me too, just in case.

I turned off the lights, climbed out the window, and saw Josiah crouched down on the side of the house. Without a second thought, I scooped him up and ran for my life. I had no clue where I was going, but I had to get the hell up out of here. I'm not sure how long I ran, but I did until I came across an old gas station. It was still open, so I went to one of the outside bathrooms and locked us inside.

Thankfully, the phone I took was a little prepaid one that didn't require a password. I dialed the one person I knew would pick up anytime I called.

"Who is this?"

"Sincere! It's me! I need you to come and get us, please!" I cried as soon as I heard his voice. No matter what, he was there despite our personal bullshit we had going on.

"Where are you? Where's Jo? Is he okay?" he rambled, and I could hear his tires screeching in the background.

"Uhm, I'm not sure. All I know is that I'm at an old Uncle Bud's in a kind of deserted area."

"Where's JO?" he repeated his previous question.

"He's right here, Sincere. He's fine, I—"

Suddenly, the room started spinning and I was hot. There was an excruciating pain in my chest and my swollen eye was throbbing. I felt some hot liquid trickle down the back of my neck. I reached back and felt it; it was blood. My breathing began to quicken, so I slid down the wall and fell to the disgusting, pissy floor. Josiah reached out and touched my face with fear in his eyes.

"Mommy, what's wrong? You okay?"

I could feel my eyes growing heavy, but the expression on Josiah's face made me fight to keep them open. With what little strength I had, I pulled the phone back up to my ear and heard Sincere yelling my name.

"Jersey! What's going on? Talk to me!"

"I... I'm trying not to slip away, Sincere. I... I need you to hurry," I stuttered.

"I need you to stay with me, Jay! Stay with me! Can you remember any street names or something close to you?"

"I... I think I saw 5th Avenue right before I got here."

"I know exactly where you are. Stay with me. I'll be there in five minutes. Put the phone on speaker phone so I can talk to Jo," he demanded. "Jo? You okay, little man?"

"Sin, I scared. Mo... mommy not wook (look) good. Her face wook (look) bad," Jo whimpered and scooted closer to me.

"It's okay, man. I'm coming to get y'all, okay? Stay close to mama and don't let her fall asleep. How about we sing her that new song you like?" I listened as they sung about ABC's and 123's. By the time the song was over, I could hear Sincere's car pull up outside.

"We're in the women's bathroom outside," I informed him and told Jo to unlock the door. A few seconds later, Sincere burst through the door and Jo ran to him and wrapped himself around his legs. Another man appeared behind him with a concerned expression. Sincere picked Jo up and held him tightly.

"You found us," Jo said as he sat up to look at Sincere, who had tears streaming down his face.

"I will always find you, Jo. Never forget that," he whispered, then kissed his cheek. "This here is my friend, Tate. He's going to take you to the car while I help mommy."

Tate took Jo from Sincere and exited out the bathroom. Leaning down, Sincere lifted my body from the ground and carried me to the car in silence. I couldn't read his face, so I had no clue what he was thinking. I had so much going through my mind that I didn't even bother to ask. I was just thankful that he was here. Carefully, he placed me in the back with Jo and sat beside me.

"Take us to Frankie's," he instructed Tate.

I laid my head back on the seat and let the tears fall as I thanked God for sparing my life yet again. He had to have a purpose for me to get out safely; even after all the bad shit I had done. I was beyond thankful.

"Don't worry about any of this shit. It's going to get handled," Sincere spoke up without even glancing my way. I nodded my head, but his words went through one ear and out the other. He had to be crazy to think I was just going to let him deal with it. I wanted Tameika so bad I could taste her, and I had every intention of making sure I would be the one to get her. She thought I would run and hide, but that was far from the truth. I was going to get that bitch for all the pain she'd caused me. That was a promise.

2

ROMAN SMILEY

I woke up to see that Amari's side of the bed was empty. When I came in last night, she was knocked out and I didn't want to wake her, so I showered and cuddled up behind her. I had no intention of going to sleep, just in case Sin called but apparently, that didn't happen. I rolled over and the clock said it was the afternoon. Damn. I didn't mean to sleep that late, but I slept good as hell.

Getting up, I stretched and went to relieve myself. After I washed my hands, I checked my phone and saw I had a few messages from Sin. I let out a sigh of relief and smiled as I examined the pictures of Jersey and Josiah asleep at his crib. Jersey was bandaged up and looked rough, but safe. I felt a little guilty for not staying out and helping, but I was thankful that he found them. Now, it wasn't all bad news I had to deliver.

I put my phone on the charger and went to find Amari. I found her in the sitting room, sipping some green tea while reading a book. When she noticed me standing there, she rolled her eyes so hard that I knew they would get stuck. I had no clue what she was upset about.

"What's with the eye rollin', ma? You not happy to see I came home early?" I quizzed with a raised brow as I sat on the opposite couch and kicked my feet up. Her little mean ass ignored me with a scowl etched on her beautiful face and lips poked out, reminding me of Jo. I had to laugh at her spoiled ass, which only made things worse. Before I could react, she sent the book flying at my head and I ducked just in time.

"What the fuck your little mean ass trying to do? Take my head off?" I barked with wide eyes.

"Where were you last night?" she interrogated.

"It's a long story, ma." I sighed as I rubbed my hands down my face.

"You were so busy you couldn't answer any of my calls? Not even one?" she yelled with tears in her eyes. The way her face was beet red and her chest was heaving up and down told me her little tantrum stemmed from more than me not answering the phone. Getting up, I went and sat on the couch beside her. She tried to get up and move away, but I grabbed her shirt and pulled her into my lap. Like the stubborn woman she is, she sat there with her arms folded across her bosom with her back facing me.

"Look at me, Amari," I stated, and she refused. "That wasn't an option. Look at me, ma," I demanded with authority. The boom of my voice made her jump a little, but she obeyed. When she turned around, her beautiful face was soaking wet and she broke down into a full-blown sob. Her shoulders were jumping up and down as she tried to control her breathing. It was pulling at my heartstrings watching my baby break down like this. She was always trying to be so strong, but I knew the one person who could make her break down like this. Kendrick.

"Come here, baby." I pulled her into my body and she laid her head on my shoulder. I kissed her forehead and rubbed her back. "It's okay, ma. Let it all out."

"He... he almost died again, Roman," she started explaining between sobs. "One minute, Frankie was saying he might wake up tomorrow and the next, Ken flatlined and had two seizures back to back. Why is so much shit happening?"

"Is he okay now?"

"Yes. They could revive him, but Frankie said it may take longer for him to wake up. I just want my brother back, Roman. It's going on two months and he still hasn't woken up. Not only do I need him, but Keyana and Hayden do too. God can't take him away."

I hated seeing her like this, and I felt guilty for not being there for her when she needed me the most. She was right; so much shit was happening, and to the same people. It was like no one could catch a break. The two people she was closest to kept getting hit the hardest, and it was taking a toll on her. I guess we went to Jamaica a little too soon.

"Kendrick is a fighter, Amari. He has a purpose because he's still here. I know it's hard, but don't dwell on all the negative things going on around you, ma. There's also positive things, like your shop reopening and us." That got a smile from her.

"It's just so hard sometimes. Ken isn't up to see all the good things, which makes them a little less exciting for me. No offense, babe."

"None taken. I understand where you're coming from. I would be like this if it was Sin," I honestly said. It was true. Sin was my brother, and I know I would be sick as fuck if something happened to him.

"Speaking of Sin, what happened on the trip?" Amari asked as she laid out on the couch and propped her feet on my lap. I started massaging one and debated on whether I should tell her what went down. Since Jersey and Jo were safe, I didn't see the harm. It would kind of be good news, right?

I told her everything, from when we got there to when Sin texted me a few hours ago. She cried, but not hard. She was just thankful they were okay. I was too. Now, all we had to worry about was keeping them safe.

"Thank you for helping him look for them. I don't know what I would have done if he didn't find them."

"You know I got you and whoever you love. I've grown to love your family like my own, so I would do whatever to keep them safe. Plus, I hated seeing Sin so messed up like that," I confessed and laid on the couch behind her. She turned and faced me with our legs intertwined. Grasping her chin, I pecked her lips a few times, causing her to giggle. "That's what I like to hear. I hate it when you cry, ma. Real shit."

"And I hate crying, but it seems like that's all I've been doing lately."

"Because you have all the reasons to cry. Crying can be good. It cleanses the soul. Just know I'm here to wipe your tears away and put a smile on your face. Even if it's just temporarily, I'll do whatever I can until it's permanent. You're my number one priority, ma. I refuse to fail you."

I meant every word of what I said. I loved this woman with all my heart. Her happiness was my happiness. I knew I wasn't God, but I would do anything to keep her happy. Anything. She was extremely special to me. Ole mean ass.

"What did I do to deserve you?" Amari cooed while gazing at me with those gorgeous, bright orbs.

"Politely dismissed my ass at the club," I joked, and she cracked up laughing.

"I could read right through you, Roman Smiley! That's why!" She giggled. "You just wanted some booty."

"Maybe," I admitted with a shrug, and she pinched my side.

"I knew it. You had that look like you were up to no good."

"Just like now," I breathed against her lips as I stuck my finger inside her opening. She was so caught up in our conversation that she didn't feel me move her panties to the side.

"Stoooppp," she tried to stifle her moan as she squirmed to get away. I stopped, then hit her upside the back of the head. She gasped and grilled me with her mouth slightly agape while I laughed.

"Throw another book at me again and watch what happens," I chuckled with a smirk.

"Okay." Amari got up and stomped behind the other couch. I sat up and the book came flying at my head, *again*. She stood there with her hands on her hips and a pleased smirk tugging at her glossy lips. "Now, what's gon' happen?"

"Nothing, you cool. I'll let that one slide too."

"That's what I thought," she mouthed and started walking toward the back.

I got up and ran behind her, but her little quick ass took off into the room and closed the door. I busted through the door and stopped when I didn't see her.

"Don't be trying to hide now, girl!" I yelled out as I searched for her.

She was good because I couldn't find her anywhere. Just when I was about to give up, she jumped on my back and we fell onto the bed. I flipped her over and started tickling her everywhere until she begged for me to stop. I laid beside her as we caught our breath. She crawled over and climbed on top of me, laying her head on my chest. I'm glad her hair was in a low ponytail or it would have been all in my face. I wrapped my arms around her and squeezed lightly, then kissed the top of her head. I lived for moments like this with her; it's what made me look forward to coming home to her.

"Move in with me," I blurted what had been on my mind for a while now. "It only makes sense, ma. You're here 99% of the time. Why not?"

"To be honest with you, I feel like I already live here. I consider it homes," she expressed, and I knew she could hear my heartbeat quicken with excitement. "I'll move in, but I want to keep my house too. It was my first home I got on my own, and I'm not ready to part with it fully yet."

"I can dig it. This my first spot too, so when we get married and start a family, we can have this as backup too. We'll need a bigger house once we expand," I explained the future I saw with her. I thought about this shit every day, and I got excited just thinking about where life would take us. Amari had come in and done a number on my heart, for real.

"It may be a little sooner than we thought," she whispered so low against my chest that I thought my ears were playing tricks on me. Was she saying...

"You pregnant, ma?"

"I... I'm not sure, but I think I am. I've been super emotional, tired, my period is late… all the signs are there. I'm just scared to take a test."

"Why?"

"Are we ready for a baby? Is it too early to be bringing someone else into this relationship when it's still fresh and new? I don't want anything to ruin the one good thing that's going right in my life right now."

"Do you love me, ma?"

"Yes."

"Do you trust me?"

"Of course."

"Then stop worrying. If you are pregnant, then it's all a part of God's plan. You know I'm not the holiest person, but I do believe that God does things for a reason. You and I are meant to be, Amari. So, if it's time to start a family, then it's time to start a family. I don't give a fuck how fast we're moving. I know that I want you and only you, ma. Believe that."

"Bushel and a peck."

"Hug around the neck," I said back. "I'm not going to rush you to take a test. Just let me know when you're ready and I'll be right there holding your hand. I got you."

We climbed under the covers for a nap and soon, Amari was out like a light. I couldn't sleep from my mind racing. To be real, I was praying that Amari was pregnant. That would give me more ammunition and courage to ask her dad for her hand in marriage. I was old school and I knew that's what Ma would expect out of me. All I could do was pray that he approved.

~&~

Amari and Lola were keeping Jersey and Jo company while Sin and I went to meet with Tate to see if he had any information for us. Jersey repeated the story about what went down to us and when she told us what she done to Vic, we knew they would come looking for her. So, we had to find them before they found her again.

"Have you talked to Kacey about all this?" I questioned Sin as I switched lanes.

"Yeah. She says she's cool with Jersey being there, but I know different. She doesn't like that shit one bit. It's all in her voice," he explained with an exasperated sigh.

"Y'all ain't together though, right?"

"Nah, we just kickin' it, but the feelings are there. I can feel it."

"You need to make a decision, bruh," I noted.

"About what?"

"About who the fuck you want to be with, nigga. Don't be leading Kacey on when you know you still love Jersey."

"I'm not leading her on, Ro. She knows what we are and where we stand."

"You sure about that? Because if she's getting mad, then I don't think she understands." I knew I was getting on his nerves, but I was just trying to help him out.

"We've talked about it. I got it, man," he snapped.

"Damn, aight. I'm just trying to help your light bright ass out, pretty boy."

"I hear ya," was all he said as he looked out the window. We were silent the rest of the ride until we got to Tate's.

Tate explained that Vic was Tameika's boyfriend that she had met while in prison. They were pen-pals at first, but things started getting serious. Long story short, they were working together to get Josiah back and kill Jersey. He didn't have a location on them, but saw that they went to *St Vincent's Birmingham*, so they had to be in that area. Tate promised to have more information soon. We didn't leave with the answers we wanted, but at least we left with more than we came with.

"You cool with stoppin' by Ma's house? I need to holla at her about something while I'm on this side of town," I ran by Sin, and he agreed.

"Nah, I don't mind. I know she's going to get in my ass about not coming to see her lately. I miss her," he expressed.

I took the next right and a few minutes later, we pulled up at Ma's house.

"Ma!" I called out as I unlocked the door. "Where you at?"

"In the kitchen," she shouted back. Sin and I made our way through the house and went to the kitchen, where she was icing a red velvet cake. My mouth immediately started watering as I watched her spread her homemade cream cheese icing over it. I had to take at least half the cake home.

"You might as well cut half of that for me," I made my presence known. Ma didn't even look up, so she didn't see Sin standing there with me.

"You better be glad I love you, boy. Yours is over there in that container. I was going to bring it by, but I... oh my goodness! You finally came to see your old Ma Dukes, huh?" Ma cooed as she walked to Sin with open arms. He tightly embraced her back as I got comfortable at the table. "About damn time!"

"Yeah, about damn time!" I instigated with a laugh.

"I'm sorry, Ma Dukes. Shit been crazy lately," Sin sighed as he sat down next to me while hitting the back of my head.

"I have all day. I want to hear everything," Ma said as she washed her hands.

Sin and I told her everything, not leaving out too many details. We trusted Ma with our lives and knew she would give us the best advice without judging us. It felt like old times. Just the three of us sitting back and talking about life. It was about time we added our ladies in the mix of this. Well, mine anyway. Sin still had some soul searching to do.

"Sounds like you got a crazy one on your hands, Sincere." Ma giggled. "I see you love her, though, if you're stepping up to the plate and taking care of her child. That's a big responsibility, baby. Something most men wouldn't do."

"See, that's what I told him. He doesn't need to be leading Kacey on," I chimed in.

"I don't think he's leading her on, Roman. It's not like he's sitting here expressing his feelings for her and jumping into another relationship. He just needs a friend to keep his mind off everything," Ma explained, defending Sin. I could see where they were coming from.

"Thank you!" Sin yelled with his arms in the air.

"Shut up, nigga."

"Don't be mad because Ma Dukes always on my side. She even said you had to split that red velvet cake with me too," he joked.

"Nah, I ain't hear all that during the conversation."

"I did."

"It's okay, Sincere. You can take this one home and I'll make another since Roman wants to be selfish," Ma stated.

"You know how I am about my cake, especially red velvet," I said, then paused. "Ma?"

"Yes, son?"

"I think I want to propose to Amari. No, scratch that. I know I want to propose to her, but I want to get your opinion on it," I explained, leaving her and Sin with their mouths wide open. I looked back and forth between the two of them with a scowl on my face. "Why y'all lookin' like that?"

"Are you serious, Roman?" Ma gasped with her hand over her heart.

"I wouldn't have said it if I wasn't," I chuckled.

"I say go for it, bruh. You and sis are one of a kind. I love y'all together and honestly, I think she's good for you. You would be crazy as hell to let her go. You know I support whatever decision you decide to make," Sin approved while embracing me in a brotherly hug. "Plus, sis crazy. I don't think you could get rid of her if you tried," he added, and we shared a laugh.

Ma was still standing there with her hand over her heart, gazing at me with tight lips and glossy, tear-filled eyes.

"You good, Ma Dukes?" Sin asked.

She just nodded her head as the tears finally hit her cheeks and rolled down them. I got up and went over to her, wrapping my arms around her. I didn't know if these were good or bad tears.

"Tell me what you thinkin', Ma. I can't read silence," I joked.

"I'm just so happy you finally found the one for you, son. You know I approve of Amari. I told you from the beginning that she's different from the other ones. I'm glad you see what I see now," she approved with a smile while hugging me back.

Ma's opinion was very important to me, and to know that she approved was music to my ears. I was happier than a muthafucka right now, and no one could change that. Now, all I had to do was ask Julian for her hand in marriage. I wasn't in a rush since Ken was still in a coma. I wanted the moment to be special, and for everyone we love to be a part of it. For that, I could take my time and pick out the perfect ring for her. Mrs. Amari White-Smiley. That has a ring to it.

HARMONY KNIGHT

"Aaahhh!" I woke up to pain shooting throughout my woman part. I struggled to open my eyes because they were throbbing, but I managed. There was heavy panting, and I felt sweat drip onto my forehead. The pain in my pussy was horrific, and I knew Warren was raping me yet again. I wanted to beg him to stop and let me go, but I didn't think I could take another one of his beatings.

"Fuuuccckkk," he groaned as he shot his seeds into me. He laid his sweaty body on top of mine as he caught his breath.

"Don't lay on the baby," I whispered.

"Bitch, you and I both know that baby is dead. Now, shut the fuck up before I knock you the fuck out. Didn't I tell you not to talk?"

I gulped loudly and did as I was told. I was scared for my life and feared what Warren could do to me. The night he kidnapped me, I woke up to bleeding between my legs. I wasn't ready to face the truth. I moved my belly until it hurt. There was no movement. Not one kick. I was devastated for the death of the life growing inside of me. I had grown so attached to the baby, only for his/her own father to take them away from me. I was to blame also. I didn't take care of my body like I knew I was supposed to. I was so caught up in trying to make my life perfect that I neglected the baby at times. I was paying for it now. Karma was a bitch and she was putting in overtime on me.

Being cooped up in this small ass one-bedroom apartment, chained to a bed gave me a lot of time to do some soul searching. God knows I missed my children and wished I could see their sweet little faces. I hadn't been the perfect mother, but I'd always done the best I could when I wasn't thinking about myself. I would have visions of Keyana and Hayden interacting with the new baby and cry. I made a vow that I would be the mother they deserved, and the one I knew I could be. My babies needed me, but I needed them a whole lot more.

My body was filled with regret as I thought of all the things I'd done to hurt Kendrick. I never had a reason to step out on him. I just did it because I knew I could get away with it. Now, that I was reaping the consequences, I realized how much of a mistake that was. What's done in the dark comes to the light, and everything blew up in my fuckin' face. If I could go back in time and change all the shit I'd done to him, I would. Kendrick deserved so much more than what I gave him, and he knew it. Yet, he chose to stick around and deal with it because he loved me. I can admit that he loved me more than I did him because you don't do the shit I did to someone you love. Damn! Why did it take me so long to realize that?

Praying had become a constant thing in my life the past few days. I've talked to God more than I have in a long time. I knew He was listening, but I felt guilty for coming to Him now when I was in a situation I couldn't get myself out of. I found myself praying almost every second, asking God to get me to my kids safely, and for Kendrick to pull through. Not knowing the status of his health was another thing that weighed heavily on me, but what could I do but pray?

Detrix came to mind, and I wondered if he went out looking for me. I hated to drag him into my mess, especially with him being away from home in unfamiliar territory. I wouldn't even be mad if he left. I wasn't his responsibility, and we were only friends with benefits. Let me stop lying; I would be livid, but understanding.

Warren finally got up and dragged his feet to the small desk that had the key to the lock holding me hostage. I was shocked when he came over and freed me, but I didn't move. I wasn't sure what he was up to, so I had to make my moves carefully.

"Get the fuck up and go shower. You got it smellin' like fish in this little ass room," he barked while jerking me up by my arm. I couldn't move fast due to the cuts and bruises over my body; also, the pain in between my thighs. "Hurry your fat ass up!"

He shoved me into the bathroom and slammed the door, locking it from the outside. Shit! I observed the bathroom and saw a window that was boarded up with wood. I couldn't believe the extreme he was going to just to keep me hostage. It wasn't like I could fit through it anyway.

I stripped from the worn, tattered clothes I had on and stepped into the shower. I winced in pain as the water rained down on my body and into open wounds. It hurt and felt good all at the same time. While I showered, I continued to observe the bathroom in search of something that could be beneficial to my escape. Nothing. Warren was a few steps ahead of me, but I wasn't going to let him win. I wanted to live longer.

"Aye! What the fuck you in here doing?" he snarled, and I heard the door open. I rinsed the soap from my body and turned the water off. I pulled the curtain back to find him standing there with a bottle of gin in his hand; his favorite pastime.

For the first time in a while, I got a good look at Warren and noticed how different he looked. He had lost weight and muscle, making him look ill. His skin was dull and he was in desperate need of a haircut and lineup. He had big, dark rings around his once sensual brown orbs. They weren't the same anymore. They were black, almost evil looking. The bottle in his hand had a lot to do with it.

"You got a problem, Harmony?" he asked as he took a nice swig from the bottle. The clear liquid didn't even burn his throat or make him wince. It was like water to him.

"Why are you doing this to me?" I whispered in fear. I wrapped the towel around my body and stepped out of the tub, never taking my eyes off him. "What did I do to you?"

"Tsk. Tsk. You really don't know why?"

I shook my head no. The way he was pacing back and forth between the small doorway frightened me. He was lowly laughing to himself while shaking his head. The liquor had him going crazy.

"Because, Harmony. Like any other woman, you chose him over me. I wanted you first, but *Kendrick* had to get to you before I did," he explained with anger lacing his tone.

Wait, what? I know he didn't say what I think he did.

"You wanted me first?" I clarified.

"Ain't that what the fuck I just said? I wanted your fat ass first, but he got to you before I could make my move. He was always in competition with me for some reason, but it looks like I won."

I couldn't believe this was all over some petty inside beef he had with Kendrick. Only little ass boys get mad and plot some revenge type shit over things like this. All because he wanted me first, ha! He should have approached me before Ken did, then maybe neither one of us would be in this predicament. I wanted him too and that's why I cheated with him. Knowing the true meaning behind his motives was fucked up. He used me.

"You used me to get back at him?"

"At first, that's how I saw things. You were just a pawn in my little game. I wanted to hit him where it hurt. Now, it's all on you," he expressed and stopped pacing to glare at me. He downed some more gin, then wiped his mouth before continuing, "I thought you would leave him, Harmony. I thought you would leave him to be with me. But, nope! You continued to string me along and play with my emotions in the process."

"Wh... what are you talkin' about, Warren? I never strung you along. My feelings and intentions with you were true," I defended myself.

"Don't give me that bullshit! If they were, then you would have left him instead of beggin' to be back in his good graces! When he found out about us, that was your chance to be free and be with me! Still, you were sniffin' up behind his ass, beggin' for your family back when we were startin' one!" He barged over to me and tightly gripped my neck, then pinned me up against the wall. The overbearing stench of alcohol made me want to puke all over him. "You're a conniving, lyin' ass bitch that deserves to rot in hell."

"Please, Warren. Don't kill me," I begged from my life. "You already took my baby from me. I'm sorry, I swear I am."

"Sorry doesn't mean a got damn thing to me! You played with my life, so now, I get to play with yours." A sinister laugh escaped his lips as his grip tightened, and he set the bottle down. He pulled a blade from behind his back and I wanted to faint. What did he plan on doing with that? With a crazed glare in his eyes, he slowly licked the blade, then slid it across my face but it didn't cut me. I was trembling and speechless. Warren was real deal psycho.

"Warren, please. Don't do this."

"Killing you will be too easy. I want you to suffer, Harmony. Suffer just like me."

"Aaahhh!" I screamed as I felt the sharp blade cut open the skin on my arm. My screams and pleas fell upon deaf ears as Warren continued to cut open different areas of my arm. I didn't know what was worse; the pain from the cuts or the tight grip that remained on my neck. When I saw him lift the blood-covered blade, something came over me. With my good arm, I punched him in the jaw, then took my foot and kicked him in the balls. He hovered over, dropping me and the blade in the process. Thinking quick and ignoring the pain, I hopped over him and grabbed the blade off the floor.

I turned around just in time to see Warren coming toward me. Closing my eyes, I swung and felt the blade pierce through his body. He gasped loudly and I heard him fall to his knees. I backed into the wall with my eyes still closed and slid down the wall. I was anticipating his comeback, but it never happened. Seconds later, I peeked my eyes open to find him laying on his back with the blade sticking up from his throat; lifeless. I couldn't believe I had just killed someone. His blood was on my hands, and there was no going back. This was not supposed to happen. How did an affair go from sex to this? This was too much, even for me. God, why did I do this!

I had to get out of here, but how without looking suspicious? I tried standing up, but fell right back down. I was weak and I could feel myself drifting. Damnit! *Come on, Harmony! Get help! Bingo!*

With what little strength I could muster up, I pulled my body across the bathroom floor until I reached Warren's body. I searched around in his pockets until I retrieved his prepaid phone. My vision was blurry and my hands were shaky as I operated the phone. *Almost done, Harmony! Don't give in just yet...*

"911, what's your emergency?"

"I... I've been raped... and attacked... please... send..."

MARISSA "RISSA" HOLDEN

Rissa's Delights was doing great things. Business was booming and the cash flow was coming in nicely. I was so thankful for how well everything was going. This had always been a dream of mine, and it was amazing seeing it come to life. I prayed over my business daily. This was something I wanted to pass down to my children in the future. I wanted nothing but growth and more success from here. More dreams and goals had come into my vision, so I was going to accomplish them one by one, even if it took the rest of my life.

"Marissa, your phone is ringing," my assistant informed me.

"Who is it?"

"Amari White."

I told my cashier I would be right back and went to my office. My phone had stopped ringing and a text came through. It was from Amari too. I didn't open it. Instead, I called her back to be sent straight to the voicemail. At first, I thought it was by accident, but when I called back a second time, I got the same result. *I guess I have no choice but to check the message.*

Amari White: Need to discuss some things with you. Dinner tonight at 8? Olive Garden?

Me: Sounds good. See you then.

What was that about? I don't know if I was paranoid, but her text seemed dry. Of course, my first thought was trying to figure out if she knew about Frankie and me. We had been trying to be low key, but the closer we got, the harder it got. I caught myself gazing and smiling at him when he came to check on Kendrick. I would catch myself before anyone noticed; I think. Damn. Was I getting myself caught up?

Me: Can you talk?

I leaned against my desk, biting away at my nails while waiting for a text back.

Frankie: You know I always have time for you.

A smirk tugged at my lips as I hit the call button next to his name.

"Hello, beautiful." His smooth baritone voice vibrated in my ear, sending a tingling sensation down my spine. It was amazing the effects this man had on my body.

"Hello, Doctor." I giggled. "How's work?"

"Busy today, but it's starting to slow down. What about you? I know business is over there booming," he complimented. "You need to bring me something sweet, and I'm not talkin' about food."

Why did he have to say that? I was happy I had a small restroom in my office so I could wash away the evidence of what he was doing to me. We had yet to have sex, but oh, was my body craving him. He loved making slick remarks like the one he just made. He loved seeing my reaction; how I would get nervous. My hands would get clammy, so I would run them together and I would stutter. Frankie thought it was cute, but it wasn't. More like embarrassing.

"No, silly," I downplayed it. "I need to ask you something," I stated in a serious tone.

"What is it? Is everything okay, Marissa?" he asked in concern.

"Amari wants to meet up to talk tonight. I... I don't know, but I kind of have a bad feeling about it. Do you think she knows about us?"

"I doubt it, baby. I think you're just being paranoid. She probably just needs someone to talk to about how she's feeling about Kendrick and feels you are the best choice. Don't look so deep into things," he explained his point of view, and it put my heart at ease. He was right. I was so wrapped up in the thought of being caught up that I didn't think about anything else. Frankie was probably right. She just needed to vent, and I was ready to be a listening ear.

"You're right, baby. I'm sorry for interrupting your day with my foolish thoughts. I'm just so scared for the truth to come out," I admitted with a sigh of relief. I noticed Frankie was silent, so I cleared my throat. "You still there?"

"Yeah. Now, I need to ask you something."

Oh, shit. "Ask away."

"What's going to happen when the truth does come out?"

"Uhm, I'm not really sure how to answer that, Frankie."

"I need to know, Marissa, because to be real, I'm gettin' tired of this secretive shit. I'm into you and I want you to be my woman, straight up. I know it's fucked up in a way, but it is what it is. We're both grown, so we can do what we want. I'm tired of going to each other's houses or driving to the next city to go on a date. It's not like you're married or you and Kendrick made things official. Y'all were simply gettin' to know each other," he expressed in an even tone. "If you're not ready to woman up and tell his family what's real, then I don't think we need to continue with what we have going on. Regardless of your decision, I'm requesting that one of the other doctors takes over for Kendrick. I can't keep doing it."

I knew this conversation was coming, I just didn't think it would be so soon. I couldn't be upset with Frankie for wanting to know where my head was at because I wanted the same at first. Knowing that he wanted to make things official had me feeling all bubbly and giddy inside. It had been a while since a man wanted to stake his claim on me; only because I never want to give one the time of day. Everything changed with Kendrick first, but Frankie was the main reason.

"Are you trying to say you want me to tell Amari tonight?"

"I'm saying it's up to you on whether I stick around or not. The ball is in your court," he said. "They're paging me. I need to go. Let me know what you decide to do."

"Okay," I whispered and hung up. I plopped down in my chair and laid my head down on my desk. Why did I choose to continue making my situation messier? Why didn't I just leave when he left the door open for me to go? I only had a few hours to make my decision when I needed a lifetime.

"Marissaaaa!" I heard Olivia's loud voice echo before she waltzed into my office. "Hey, best!"

"Hey," I replied dryly without lifting my head up from my desk. I wasn't in the mood for her, but I knew that wasn't going to matter to her.

"Ooo, bih! Don't do that!" she spat dramatically. "What's wrong with you?"

"Nothing," I sighed, looking up at her. Her facial expression told me she knew I was lying, so I laid my head back down, only for her to pick it back up again.

"Lies! You know you can't lie to me," she called me out with a smirk, which made me crack a smile. She knew me too well.

"I'm in a sticky situation, Olivia. I don't know what to do," I groaned while slumping down in my chair.

"About?" I gave her a knowing look, and she knew exactly what I was talking about. "Frankie and Kendrick?"

"Yes! Frankie just basically gave me an ultimatum. Either I tell Kendrick's family about us or he's going his own way. Amari called and she wants to have dinner tonight so we can talk, and he wants me to tell her then. I kind of think she already knows; I'm not really sure. What I do know is that I don't know what to do!" I rambled, on the verge of tears. I was so overwhelmed with everything going on, and I couldn't blame anyone but myself.

"I don't blame Frankie! I would do the same. Listen, Rissa. You're my girl and you know I love you, so I'm only going to keep it real with you. You owe it to Frankie to decide, and you owe it to Kendrick's family as well. You've been playing a dangerous game, best. Tell me, have you just sat down and thought about the choices you have made in this situation you created?"

"No, I haven't," I mumbled honestly.

"Well, sit there and do that while I go get some pecan pie. Maybe you'll see what I see," she demanded and whisked away, leaving me there with my thoughts.

I knew my actions came with consequences, but I didn't think I would have to face them so soon. Olivia was correct; I was playing a dangerous game. Over the time Ken has been in a coma, I'd gotten to know his family very well and they were super close. Not having a close relationship with anyone but my mother and grandmother is what drew me into the Whites and made me keep my secret longer. It wasn't fair to anyone that I was being selfish with my decision. I wanted my cake and to eat it too; well, I was eating it. I had to stop being greedy and satisfying the hunger for it deep inside of me. Damn, this was going to be hard, but I had to do it.

"So, did you think about it?" Olivia quizzed with wide eyes and a mouth full of pie. She closed the door with her foot and sat down at my desk, placing her plate on top of it. "I hope you did."

"I did." I answered.

"And?" She glanced up at me with questionable eyes.

"I know what I'm going to do."

~&~

I hated running late. After lunch with Olivia, I finished my day up at the shop and came home to take a quick nap. Well, that quick nap was a little longer than I thought. It was now going on 8:15 p.m., and I was supposed to meet Amari at eight. When I woke up, I shot her a quick text, informing her of my late arrival and said I would get there ASAP. I handled my hygiene and dressed comfortably since we were meeting at *Hattie B's Hot Chicken*. I unwrapped my hair, put on a little makeup, and scurried out the door.

It took me ten minutes to make it to the restaurant, but I made it. When I found Amari, she was sitting at a table far in the back and was already eating. I couldn't even get upset because if the tables were turned and she was the one thirty minutes late, I would be chowing down too. My stomach growled and I wanted to go order my food, but since I was already late, I decided to sit down and wait.

"I'm so sorry I'm late," I apologized as I sat down in the chair across from her. "I slept way longer than I intended to."

"It's fine," Amari replied with no emotion. I couldn't read her and that bothered me. Any other time she greeted me, it was cheerful and warm. Now, it was dull and dry. Shady, kind of. She didn't even look up as she continued to finish her meal. The awkward silence was killing me, so I scrolled through my email to send out confirmation letters to orders for the upcoming week. Five minutes passed before Amari cleared her throat to gain my attention.

Our eyes met and I shivered from how cold hers were. Her usual glowing green eyes were a darkish, bluish color; like the depth of the sea. Her expression was blank and her head was tilted to the side as she just glared at me, making me extremely uncomfortable. I sat patiently, waiting for her to say something because I damn sure didn't know what to say.

"Y'all fuckin'?" she interrogated, coming at me in an unexpected manner. I was shocked and speechless. I didn't quite know how to answer that question because it wasn't something I was normally asked. My gut feeling was true; she knew. It was the confirmation I needed to know I was making the right decision.

"Excuse me?" I played dumb to get her to rephrase the question.

"Cut the bullshit, Marissa. You know what I'm talkin' about. Are you and Frankie fuckin'? Yes or no?"

"No, we are not." I wasn't lying.

"Then what the fuck y'all got going on? Don't say nothing because I know I'm not dumb and I know what I've been seeing." She got a little loud, causing other people to look our way. She snarled her nose up and rolled her eyes at them, then reverted her attention back to me. "Well?"

"We... uhm... we've been dating for a few weeks now. You know, seeing each other," I admitted with a shaky voice. It was hard, but it was something I had to do. "I never meant for it to happen; it just did. I'm sorry, but I chose him. I know I said I will be there for Kendrick, and I am a woman of my word. I wi—"

"What makes you think you're a woman of your word when you can't even keep it to my brother, who's in a fuckin' coma?" she snarled through gritted teeth. "You're sitting here telling me that you've been messing around with the doctor that's taking care of *my* brother? And you've been sitting in me and my family's faces, acting like shit is all sweet and dandy?"

I didn't say anything. I let my silence be the answer.

"I guess your silence tells me everything I need to know," she chuckled while throwing her napkin on the table and leaning back with her arms folded. "So, what am I supposed to tell Ken when he wakes up? Oh, the woman you thought was for you turned out to be just like Harmony? The conniving, sneaky bitch that I still owe a few ass whoopings. Is that what you want me to tell him, because it sounds damn good to me, don't you think?"

"Please, Amari. I'm so sorry. I'm only human. I... I can't control my feelings and the path life decides to take me on. Some things just happen that are out of our control."

"No, bitch! You had full control over your gotdamn actions! Don't sit here and spit that I gave into temptation shit and I'm only human! I don't give a fuck about the excuses you're spitting at me. It's cool that you're keepin' it real with me and didn't lie. I can respect that, but don't make excuses for why you did it. Just own up to the shit and keep it moving. Like I said, you're still a sneaky, conniving bitch to me; that won't change. All I have to say is stay the fuck away from us; especially Kendrick. If I catch you around then that's your ass. I don't give a fuck how much bigger you are than me. I will still wipe the floor with your ass like you're a gotdamn midget. You better be thanking Allah or whoever you praise for letting me spare your ass. I had hope in you, Marissa. I really did. You sure fooled me. I wish you and Frankie hell. I hope he breaks your heart into a million-tiny fuckin' pieces and burns them all. I want you to feel how my brother is going to feel when I tell him about the real you. Take heed to my promise, hoe."

I allowed my tears to fall freely as I let every cruel word Amari spat at me sink in. Whoever came up with the phrase *sticks and stones may break my bones, but words will never hurt me* was telling a got damn lie. Amari's words hurt me to the core; only because what she said was true. I was sneaky and conniving for what I did, but like I said, I'm only human. I can't change what I've done, and I don't think I would even if I could.

Besides the hurt, I felt relief. Relief from the truth finally coming to light and me deciding. It wasn't the easiest decision, but it was what my heart wanted. Frankie was who I wanted to be with. Now, I could give him all of me and not hold back. I couldn't wait to tell him the news.

I was going to miss visiting Kendrick and sitting with his parents. We had grown a bond that I cherished. It was going to be weird adjusting to not seeing them, but I would manage. I just prayed they would find it in their hearts to forgive me; especially Amari. Who am I kidding? She would hate me for the rest of her life.

Deciding that I was no longer hungry, I grabbed my purse to leave and go tell Frankie the news in person. Also, to finally have sex. It was the best way to celebrate for making things official. I made my way to my car, sending Frankie a text to make sure he was at home. I reached for my door handle and was met with a blow to the face. I dropped my purse and keys as I stumbled backward and fought through the pain. I looked up and Amari was standing there with a smirk tugging at her lips and her hands on her hips.

"I hope you didn't think I was going to let you get away with that shit. I owe you more than that, but I'm going to let you slide for the sake that we're out in public. Just know, if I catch you somewhere I know I won't get arrested, I'm in that ass," she threatened and bumped into me as she went to her car. I guess I had that coming.

Shaking it off, I watched her leave, then got into my car. I checked my face and figured a bruise would show up in the morning, but nothing makeup couldn't cover. I was just happy it was all over and Frankie and I could move on in one peace

3

KENDRICK "KEN" WHITE

*B*eep. *Beep. Beep.*

     I could hear the beeping, but my eyes wouldn't open. It was like they were glued shut and I would have to literally pry them open. I tried to lift my arm, but nothing happened. That was odd. I tried again and failed. My body felt... well, it didn't feel like anything. I couldn't feel anything. What in the hell was going on? Why couldn't I feel anything? I squeezed my eyes tight, then popped them open as hard as I could. I blinked for a moment to adjust to my surroundings. The first thing I saw made me smile. Mari was sitting up in the seat beside the window, knocked out with Keyana and Hayden curled under her. They were asleep also, which made me wonder what time it was. The sun was out, so I assumed it was morning.

The wonderful aroma of Starbucks coffee filled my nostrils and just by the smell, I knew it was for Mari. I had gotten it for her many times, so I was familiar with it. The door opened and in walked Roman with a cup holder that held four drinks and fast food bags in his hands. He closed the door and turned toward me, dropping the food in the process.

"Oh, shit," he cussed in surprise. "You... uh... let me get the doctor." He set the cup holder down and bent down to pick up the food, placing it beside the cup holder. He jogged out the room and moments later, came back with a short, mixed doctor.

"Hello, Kendrick. It's nice to have you back with us," she greeted cheerfully. "I'm Dr. Kennings. How are you feeling?"

"I... I need some water," I managed to get out in a raspy voice. My throat was drier than the Sahara Desert.

"Let me go get you some water and my nurse. I'll be right back," Dr. Kennings stated and walked away. My attention went to Roman, who was waking Mari up. I watched as her sleepy eyes fluttered open and she gazed at him with a warm smile. She was in love. I could see it all over her face. The way she looked at him and how she was glowing were dead giveaways. Apparently, I had missed a few things while I was out and I couldn't wait to hear all about it.

Roman whispered something in her ear, and that's when she turned her head and our eyes met. Her mouth dropped slightly and eyes identical to mine became tear-filled. I gave her a weak smile and tried to reach out for her. Still, I couldn't move. At first, I thought it was because I had just woken up and the blood needed to flow through my body. Now, I was second guessing that thought.

"Kendrick!" Amari cried and ran over to me, causing Keyana and Hayden to topple over and wake up. They looked around, confused. Roman pointed my way and they rubbed the sleep from their eyes, then looked over at me. Their little faces lit up and they got up to run over to me. Mari was laying out over me, crying her eyes out, but I couldn't feel her. I felt bad because I couldn't reach out and console her. Man, something has got to give. What's going on with me?

"Daaadddyyy!" they squealed in unison and hugged whatever part of me Mari wasn't laying on. Seeing them had me tearing up. Roman was in the corner, observing us with a smile on his face. Where were my parents?

"I'm so happy you're awake!" Mari exclaimed as she got some tissue. "I have to call Mama and Daddy."

"Sorry it took so long. I had to handle a little problem," Dr. Kennings explained as she walked into the room with a cup of water in her hand and a nurse right behind her. The nurse came over and immediately began checking my vitals. Mari scooted herself and the kids out the way as she spoke on the phone. Dr. Kennings came over, and I thought she was going to try to hand me the cup, but she brought it straight to my lips instead. Fuck.

"Is that better?" she asked as I finished the small cup.

"Yes, thank you. What's wrong with me? Why can't I move or feel anything?" I blurted, wanting answers immediately. The room fell into an awkward silence.

"Kendrick, do you remember what happened to you? I know it's a little early to be asking you since you are just waking up, but I'm curious to know," Dr. Kennings said as she looked back and forth between the chart in her hand and one of the monitors hanging on the wall. Why was she avoiding my question?

"Can you answer my question first?"

"Please, calm down. I need you to stay as calm as possible," she instructed. "For me to explain to you what's going on with you, I need you to explain to me what happened to you. That way, it will all make sense and you can ask all the questions you want."

I took her warning and calmed myself as I tried to think of my last memory. Flashbacks of Warren holding a gun played in my head. It was hard to remember anything else, but seeing him standing there was enough to let me know what happened; he shot me. I laid back and let my mind take me back to that day; from leaving the doctor's office to remembering the tingling sensation that traveled down my spine after feeling the bullet pierce through my flesh. A monitor started going crazy, so I opened my eyes and looked around.

"Did you remember?" Dr. Kennings asked.

I nodded my head yes.

"Good, but I need you to try and calm down. Your blood pressure shot up and I need it to stay down. Do you think you could tell me without getting too upset?"

"Yes." I breathed. Mari rushed back to me with concern etched on her face.

"What's wrong?" she asked the doctor while examining me.

"He remembers what happened to him and it has him a little

upset; which I can understand. We need him calm," Dr. Kennings explained.

"And how do you expect him to stay calm?" Mari snapped, like I knew she would. Roman got up and stood behind her, rubbing her shoulders and whispering something in her ear. Watching them interact made me want that for myself. That's when I thought about Marissa. Did she know? Had she been here?

"Sorry about that," Roman said to Dr. Kennings.

"No need to apologize." She brushed it off and returned her attention back to me. "We are going to step out so I can go over your vitals, and to give you time to calm down and gather your thoughts. Do you need anything?"

"Something else to drink."

"What would you like?"

"A Sprite, please."

Dr. Kennings noted it and promised her nurse would bring me one. Once they were gone, I turned my attention to Amari and was about to ask about Rissa when the door opened and my parents walked in. My mother instantly burst into tears and fell to the ground, praising God.

"My baby is up! Thank You!" she cried, and a lone tear slithered down my cheek. I can't imagine the worry and pain my family had been enduring while I was out. I was thankful. Thankful for another chance at life and being able to be with my family again. Life wasn't always promised.

Dad helped Mama up, and Mari handed her some tissues. Mama scurried over to me while Daddy stood back with Mari and kissed her forehead. He knew how mama could get about us, so he always let her have her time first. I admired my dad and always wished I could be half the man, father, brother, and future husband that he is. He gave me a head nod with a smile and I did the same in return as Mama stroked my cheek. I looked around the room at the people who loved me and felt like I was missing someone; I just didn't know who.

"I'm so overjoyed to see you up, baby. How you feeling?" Mama cooed as she fixed my blankets and picked away the invisible lint. Typical mother.

"Feeling? I'm not doing much of that. I can't move. I've tried many times, but fail," I explained, looking off into the distance. It was as if saying it out loud made something in my brain click. *Please, don't tell me...* "Am I paralyzed?"

"Uhm... I think we should wait for Dr. Ken—" Mama started, but was cut off.

"Yes, son. You are," Dad sighed while looking me straight in the eyes.

"Julian!" Mama gasped.

"What, Marie? He was going to find out anyway. The boy ain't dumb. Might as well get it out in the open."

"I'm... paralyzed..." I breathed in disbelief.

"Permanently from the waist down, and temporarily from the neck to the waist," Mari explained with sympathy leaking from her tone. "I'm so sorry, Ken."

There was no need for her to apologize. She wasn't responsible for this. She wasn't the one who pulled the trigger. All over a female that was *mine*. A female that he fucked behind my back and got pregnant. Harmony was my fiancée. Harmony was the mother of my two children. We had started a life together and formed a bond. I can't lie and say I wasn't fucked up over all this because I loved the hell out of that girl, and Warren knew it. Apparently, he didn't give a fuck. I just didn't know it was that deep for him to actually attempt to kill me. Over what belonged to me. It was cool because I knew he was going to get what he had coming for him.

"Who did it?" Roman spoke for the first time in a while. He had been so silent that I forgot he was in the room.

"You know?" Dad asked, and I nodded my head. "Spit that shit out then, son!"

"It was Warren."

"Son of a bitch," Mama cussed, shocking us all.

Dad walked out of the room, and Roman was right on his heels. None of us tried to stop them. It is what it is. Karma is a bitch, and if they're the ones to deliver it to Warren, then so be it. I couldn't get him, so the closest person to me could and I knew Dad would show no mercy. He was an OG, but changed his life when I was born. Some old ways were embedded in him, and this was the perfect opportunity to put them to use.

"That's why that hoe disappeared! They probably set you up!" Mari accused. "This was all a part of their fucked up little plan!"

"Amari! Don't forget we have two children in the room," Mama reminded her of Keyana and Hayden. Shit, I can't lie. I had forgot about them too. This wasn't something we needed to discuss in front of them. Harmony was their mother, and even though we didn't say her name, they were smart enough to figure out. I would never talk down on Harm in front of them. At the end of the day, she was their mother and she was a good one; despite all the extra bullshit she had been pulling lately. I knew she loved Keyana and Hayden with everything in her.

"Shit, my bad. You said a bad word too, though." Mari mumbled and rolled her eyes. Her short ass was on ten. I could tell by the way she was moving from side to side and flexing her hands. She was ready to Rhonda Rousey Harmony's ass, so I changed the subject to get her mind off it.

"Has Marissa been around?"

"Fuck that bitch too!" Mari screamed, causing Keyana and Hayden to bust into a fit of giggles. Mama reached over and popped her on the mouth.

"What did I just say?" Mama scolded with "the look." You know, that look that all Black mama's have? All they have to do is look at you a certain way, and you automatically straighten up? Mari and I are grown as fuck, but we still know what "the look" means.

"Sorry, Mama. I'm just so pissed with her! She fooled the hell out of me."

"What do you mean, baby? Last I knew, everything was fine. She's been up here almost every day, but I do find it unusual that I haven't seen her in a few days," Mama stated. "What happened?"

"Yeah, what happened?" I repeated. Mari's reaction had me curious and worried because it wasn't what I thought it would be.

"She was messing around with Frankie. I had been noticing how friendly and comfortable they were getting around one another, so I confronted her on it and she told the truth. You see Kendrick has a new doctor, Mama."

"Wow," Mama sighed while shaking her head. "I cannot believe she would do something like that. She was such a sweet girl and the way she was here for Kendrick, I just knew she was going to be my future daughter-in-law."

"I'm confused. What was going on?" I quizzed with a frown.

I laid back and listened to Mari explain what all had transpired between them and Rissa while I was out. In the beginning, everything sounded good and had me feeling happy inside. Hearing how she was there with me day in and day out warmed my heart. It had me thinking she was down for me; that is, until I heard the rest of it.

"Damn. She did me like that?"

"And got jawed. She better be glad we were in a public place and I'm a business owner or I would have dragged her ass all up and down 7th Avenue. These bitches got me fucked up if they think they can keep playing you! I swear to gaaahhh, the next hoe that even *thinks* she can play with your heart is going to be missing hers! My ass will be like Regina from *Once Upon a Time* and snatch the bitch's heart and crumple that shit to dust. Let another one try me!" she exclaimed in annoyance.

"Excuse your aunt and her filthy mouth. She knows better," Mama griped to Keyana and Hayden.

"Ooo, Tt! You gon' get in troubleeee!" Keyana teased Mari while Hayden stood behind her snickering.

"I'm sorry, y'all," Mari apologized, avoiding Mama's glare. "Do as I say and not as I do, got it?"

"Yes ma'am."

I took a deep breath and closed my eyes. I could feel a headache coming on and just wanted peace and quiet. I can't front, I was in my feelings about Rissa. She straight played me in the worst way. She left me while I was down and out, when I needed her the most. That was fucked up and hurtful. It wasn't my fault I got shot and went into a coma. Then again, I couldn't be as mad as I wanted to. We were still in the phase of getting to know one another and hadn't put a title on us. I just thought she would have stuck it out until I woke up. I assumed we had a deeper connection, but I was wrong.

All this shit was too much on me at once. My mind was on a thousand, and I didn't think it would slow down anytime soon. I could feel eyes on me, so I squinted to see everyone looking at me. I opened them all the way and gave them a weak smile.

"Don't do that, baby. You don't have to put on a mask for us. Let us be strong for you. You've been through so much in these last few months. You can't carry all that by yourself. That's what we're here for," Mama expressed as she grabbed my hand.

"She's right, Ken. You know we got you," Mari cosigned.

Keyana and Hayden climbed up on the bed and snuggled up against me. This was exactly what I needed right now.

"What's her name?" a loud voice boomed from the hallway, causing us all to look at the door.

"Her ID says Harmony Knight, sir."

Harmony!

"Mommy!"

AMARI

"Whoa, whoa!" I exclaimed as Hayden jumped off the bed and headed for the door. I scooped him up and spun around, placing him back on the bed.

"It was Mommy!" he whined and folded his little arms across his chest. "Key said so!"

"We don't know that for sure, baby. Someone could have the same name as her. Let Tt go check it out and see, okay?"

"Okay," he grumbled with his lip poked out. He scooted closer to Kendrick and laid his head down. I looked at Mama and Ken before running out into the hallway to find out what was going on. I searched around the hall and there was no sight of anyone except for a few nurses going on break. I decided to try my luck at the nurse's station.

"How may I help you?" the nurse asked cheerfully.

"Uhm, is there a Harmony Knight here?"

"Let me check." I waited patiently as she quickly tapped away at the keyboard. Hopefully, she was already registered.

"Yes, we do. She just got here from an emergency call. It looks like she's in surgery right now," she explained. "They just took her up on the elevator."

"Do you know what happened?"

"No ma'am. I can tell you what floor she's on and you can ask to speak to someone up there for more information."

"Please."

"She's on the eighth floor. Do you know where the elevators are?"

"Yes. Thank you," I thanked her and jogged around the corners to them. I jarred at the up button and impatiently waited for the slow elevator to reach my floor. When I made it up, I was a little confused at first, but found my way to another nurse's station.

"How may I help you?"

They must have that rehearsed. "I'm here for Harmony Knight."

"One sec," she paused and picked up the phone. She had a brief conversation with someone and looked at me, "What's your name and in what relation are you to Ms. Knight?"

"Amari White and... her sister." I managed to choke through gritted teeth. There was a bitter taste in my mouth. That was the hardest thing for me to say. That bitch would never be any relation to me. Evaaa.

She continued talking before hanging up and turning her attention back to me. "Dr. Morrison will be right with you."

"Thank you."

A few seconds later, a tall, fine muscular white man in a white jacket came gliding towards me. He flashed me a gorgeous smile and I almost melted. His ass knew he was fine. I glanced down at his left hand and, of course, there was a wedding band. As sexy as he was, I bet he was fuckin' some nurses and patients; just like Frankie's slimy ass. Muthafucka.

"Hi, are you Amari White?"

"I am. How's Harmony?"

"She's a little beat up and she lost the baby, but she's going to be fine," Dr. Morrison assured me.

"Then, why is she having surgery?" I interrogated in confusion.

"Because, Ms. Knight was raped and badly beaten, and that's how the baby died. Since she was further along, Dr. Bruce had to perform a C-section. Other than that, she had a few bruised ribs and cuts scattered over her body. Still, I assure you that she will be fine and make a speedy recovery. I do mean physically. Mentally, I'm not sure how she will heal. Everyone copes differently," Dr. Morrison explained.

Is it bad that I don't feel bad for her? I'm sorry, but I don't. That bitch had all that shit and more coming to her for all the grimy shit she did. Why should I get mad at karma for doing her job? You reap what you sow, hoe.

"Who done this to her?" I faked sad. Somehow, I managed to squeeze out two tears; one from each eye. I had to make this look real, so I was playing my part well.

"A man by the name of Warren Stanley," he revealed, and I wasn't shocked. Knowing Harmony, her dumb ass done something stupid to make Warren go over the edge and try to kill her ass. Maybe he should have.

"Oh, no! Where is he now? He can't get to her!" I deserved a Grammy for this performance.

"Calm down, Ms. White. Mr. Stanley is deceased," he informed me, and I almost hit the floor. I didn't know whether to be sad that we couldn't get his ass first or happy he was no longer a problem in our lives. Like Harmony, he got his karma. He just had to pay a higher price.

I continued my little award-winning show for Dr. Morrison until Roman texted me, wanting to know where I was. I left my number with the nurse to call whenever Harmony was awake and went back down to find Roman. He was waiting for me by the elevator on Ken's floor. He reached for my hand and pulled me into him. I laid on his chest and got high from his invigorating scent. He rested his hands on the small of my back and his chin on the top of my head. We stayed like that for a few minutes, not caring that we were in the middle of a busy hallway.

Roman let me go and pressed the down button on the elevator. He led and I followed without asking questions. We made it outside and walked silently, hand in hand to a small café. I found us a place to sit while he ordered for us. The inviting smell of fresh coffee calmed me. This place was relaxing and just what I needed.

"Caramel Frappuccino with an extra shot of caramel and an apple fritter," he announced with a grin. "I know it's not Starbucks, but it's just as good. I know your other one is probably melted by now."

"What you know about a little ole place like this?" I teased as he handed me my things.

"I've had a few little chicks bring me here," he shrugged, like it was no big deal. I stood up, but he quickly sat me back down. "Chill, ma. It was a joke. Now, calm your little mean ass down before I have to act a nigga in here."

"Don't play with me, Roman. You know I won't hesitate to pop your big ass."

"Why you gotta be so mean and aggressive? Here I am, trying to be a good husband and let you get some fresh air because I know you're overwhelmed. And you want to be abusive. What did I get myself into?" he joked, faking hurt and I laughed. There he goes again, taking my mind off all the bullshit in my life and keeping me happy. Damn, I love this man.

"I'm sorry, baby. I'm just frustrated," I admitted.

"I know, ma. I am too. Real shit, your dad and I, we're going to find that pussy ass nigga. We already got some shit in rotation."

"There's no point when Warren's dead."

"Dead? How you know?"

I went on to explain the conversation I had with Dr. Morrison. I tried to hide the smile that tugged at my lips as I pictured him. Roman would kill me if he knew I was thinking about another man. I could look, but not touch. He was all the man I needed.

"Speaking of that bitch, I guess you ain't whoop her ass enough," Roman spat and sipped his smoothie.

"What do you mean?"

"I paid Tiffani a visit after what you told me. Before I set her couch on fire, she told me Harmony had come to her with the plan of burning your shop down so she could get back at you. Like a dumb ass, Tiffani went along with it, which resulted in her getting her ass beat and losing her house."

I was livid. I couldn't believe that bitch had the audacity to sabotage my business; my livelihood. Unfortunately, Harmony knew first-hand how much my business meant to me; well, she knew through Kendrick. Still, she knew and tried to take that away from me. Just because she was a big, miserable hoe that ruined her life didn't give her the right to try and do the same to me. She was just big mad because I always handed her that ass and she couldn't keep up, so she had to go below the belt. She should have known better.

"Sneaky bitch," I mumbled and got up from my chair.

"Sit down, ma. Don't even sweat that shit. You got a new shop without having to use the money the insurance company is going to give you. Look where you are and look at her; living your life is enough payback. Don't let her continue to get you riled up and act out of character. It's not going to solve anything."

"It will make me feel better," I giggled, and Roman laughed. I sat back down, pulling my chair closer to his. I locked my arm in his and laid my head on his arm.

"You listening to me, Amari?"

"Yes, Roman. I'm just taking it all in and thinking about it," I answered honestly.

"I'm just saying. You're better than that. Stop being so damn mean," he teased, nudging me with his shoulder.

"Shut up," I kissed my teeth and leaned up to find my purse. I dug around until I found what I was looking for. I closed my eyes and grasped it tightly, then faced Roman while holding it behind my back. I couldn't help the goofy grin that was tugging at my lips; it caused Roman to smile too.

"Why you lookin' like that, ma? Shit ugly as hell," he teased.

"I have something to give you, but you have to close your eyes first," I instructed.

"Hell nah! Nope. You ain't gettin' me."

"What?"

"You might steal off on me or something, with that creepy ass smile. You look like you're up to something," he explained with a serious expression, causing me to smile wider. He always thought I was trying to abuse him. His ass was too big for all that.

"Just hold your hands out and close your eyes, Roman," I demanded. He did as I asked and I placed it in his hands. "Open them."

I watched carefully as he slowly opened his eyes, and they widened in surprise. He just sat there, staring at the positive pregnancy test. My suspicions were confirmed; I was pregnant. I took a test before coming to the hospital this morning and stuck it in my purse. I wanted to wait to tell Roman after I went to the doctor, but decided against it and now seemed like the perfect time to tell him. I wanted him to experience it all with me; doctors' appointments, seeing the ultrasounds, and listening to the heartbeat. I didn't want him missing out on such an amazing experience. I wanted him right there, holding my hand every step of the way.

"Wooh!" he yelled, jumping up from the table and scaring me, along with the few people here. "I knew it! Daddy got that good aim, don't he?"

"Whatever," I giggled.

He sat back down and pulled me onto his lap. We engaged in a passionate kiss and I was on cloud nine, but I was scared it wouldn't last long. It was like every time things started looking up, something bad would happen. Ken had finally woken up and I was carrying a life inside of me I had created with the man of my dreams. Jersey and Jo were safe. Everything seemed too good to be true and I hated to admit it, but I was scared it wasn't going to last long. Only because of how crazy life had been lately.

"Real shit, I'm happy as fuck, ma. I feel like this is the beginning of a new chapter. A great one," Roman expressed as he rubbed my still flat stomach. "I can't wait until you get all big and shit. I promise to give you all the foot massages you want."

"Don't tell me that. I'm might take advantage of it." I half joked; it did sound tempting.

"Anything for my baby."

"Aaawww! Bushel and a peck," I cooed and kissed his cheek.

"Hug around the neck, but I wasn't talking about you." He snickered. "I was talking about little Rome baking in the oven."

"Rome? What makes you think it's a boy?"

"I didn't say I did. I'm just speaking things into existence," he stated and flashed me a smile. "I want a boy first, then a girl."

"Then a girl? Who said I wanted to have two kids?"

"Who said I meant by you?" he shot back, and I slapped him upside the head. As a reflex, he did the same to me with a deep frown on his face. "That shit hurt, girl."

"Well, don't play with me. Baby daddy," I giggled, being silly. I couldn't help it. I was so overwhelmed with joy about being pregnant. At first, I was having mixed feelings. It all changed when Ken woke up.

"Let's finish up so we can get back to the hospital. I want to chill with Ken before I go meet up with Sin and Tate."

"Jersey and Jo can come over with me. I don't want them alone at all."

We finished up and walked back to the hospital. Time to breathe in some fresh air was exactly what I needed. I was very appreciative of Roman and how he always put me first. He was going to be an amazing father, and I was eager to see him in action.

"When do you want to tell everyone the big news?" he asked, breaking me from my thoughts.

"I was thinking at my grand reopening. Celebrate two things at once," I suggested with a smile.

"I'm down with that, ma. Just let me know when and I'll get it set up."

"Thank you, baby."

"You good. Now, come to the car and hop on this dick. We can start celebrating early and I heard pregnant pussy is the best, so I'm ready to test that theory."

"You're so nasty." I giggled, but I was following right behind him. It was never too early to celebrate, right?

SINCERE

"Daddy? Daddy, where are we going?" My voice trembled as I sat in the backseat with my belongings next to me. He had been driving for a while, and I just wanted to know where we were going. Mama was knocked out in the passenger seat, and I knew she wasn't useful.

"Just ride, Sincere. We'll be there shortly," he answered with a hint of irritation in his tone.

"We've been riding for a while and I'm tired," I whined. "Where are you and Mommy's bags?"

"Sincere Peters, what did I just say?" he barked while glaring at me through the rear-view mirror. His eyes were redder than a candy apple with signs of weariness around them. Over time, my father had changed, just like Mama. He was now that evil, bitter man I prayed he would never be. A few months back, he came home and announced that he had gotten fired from his job due to being late more than five times. He promised to begin looking for another job, but it never happened. I watched as he slowly picked up the same habits Mama had, and that's when things changed. Life went downhill.

Moments later, we pulled up to a nice mansion and I was in awe. It was amazing, but why were we here? We didn't know anyone with enough money to afford a mansion, so I was curious to know. Daddy checked in at the gate and drove up the driveway. He parked and woke Mama from her slumber. She quickly fixed herself, checking her appearance in the mirror and poppin' some mint gum in her mouth to hide the sleep funk. They both gazed at one another and then back at me. Even at a young age, I knew my parents well and could read the sadness in their orbs. Something bad was about to happen; I could feel it.

They got out and opened the backdoors. Daddy grabbed my bags while Mama unbuckled my seatbelt and helped me out. They each took one of my hands and led me to the front door, ringing the doorbell. A short man in a suit opened and greeted us, leading us inside the enormous house. I could feel Mama shaking, and Daddy's palms were sweaty. They took slow, short strides as they followed behind the mystery man. I was afraid, but couldn't voice it. Something told me to keep my mouth closed, and that was exactly what I did.

"You may go inside. Mr. Porter is waiting for you," the man said and walked away. Daddy stood up straight and knocked on the door before opening it and leading us inside.

The inside was an office with a man, who I guessed was Mr. Porter, sitting behind a wooden desk. There were a few other men in there as well, who I assumed to be security guards or something. The way they all stood up once we entered and gathered around the sitting light-skinned man gave me that assumption. I stopped in my tracks and hid behind my father's legs, which made him stop too. Mama stayed back a little and waited to see what was going to happen.

"I've been waiting for the two of you. Where's my money?" Mr. Porter asked Daddy. Daddy glanced back at Mama, then cleared his throat to speak.

"We don't have it. Instead, we thought we could offer you something worth much more than anything we could offer," Daddy answered. Looking down at me, he pulled me off his legs and pushed me forward. I tried to run back to him, but he stopped me with his hand on my head. I started crying, but he stared straight ahead, ignoring my tears.

"Daddy, please! I want to go home," I cried, fighting him with all my strength. "Please, Daddy!"

"Is he your way of paying me?" Mr. Porter questioned.

"Yes."

"No, Daddy! I don't want to go with him. I want to stay with you and Mommy!" I pleaded. Was he really trying to give me away as a pawn? A payment? Did they really not want me anymore?

"I'm sorry, Peters. I can't take him," Mr. Porter refused. "You said you would have my money today, but instead, you bring me your one and only child. Your son, your namesake. I thought you were better than that, Peters. You're not a man of your word anymore?"

"Look, Bryce. I... I didn't have enough time. My wife and I... we... we've been trying to find work to pay you back, but shit has been hard. Now, this was a tough decision to make because I love my son more than anything in life, so we figured he would cover the expenses we owe. He's worth that and so much more," Daddy explained while crying.

"Please, Bryce. Just take him and let us be," Mama spoke for the first time.

By now, I had stopped crying and laid out on the floor. I could hear them talking, but I wasn't paying attention anymore. Something had come over me and my sadness was replaced with anger. I felt my heart turn cold and somehow, I buried all my feelings deep inside. If they wanted to give me away, then so be it. Maybe Mr. Porter would treat me better.

"Like I said, I can't do that. I gave you plenty of time to get my money to me. Now, time is up. You know what comes next," Mr. Porter hissed with a smirk tugging at his lips.

"Please, give us more time!" Mama begged.

"Too late. Fellas, I need y'all to collect my payment from Mr. and Mrs. Peters," he demanded as he rose to his feet. "It was nice doing business with you two. I'll make sure little Sin here will be in good hands. See you on the other side."

POW! POW! POW!

After witnessing my mother and father's deaths, I passed out and hours later, woke up at Ma Dukes' house. Roman was sitting beside me, waiting for me to wake up. I explained to him what I thought was a dream, but later knew that it was my reality.

"Earth to Sin! Wake up, Squanto." Roman chuckled, shaking my arm.

"Move, Ro," I demanded and stretched. "I ain't even know I had fell asleep."

"I see. Jersey and Jo were knocked out too, but Amari woke them up. Get up so we can go get up with Tate."

I got up and went to the bathroom to relieve myself and handle my hygiene. Ro, Tate, and I were going to meet up with Archie to see what info he had on Vic and Tameika. On the phone, he said it was good news, so I hoped he found their location. I was ready to off their asses so life could get back to normal. I swaggered into the living room to find Jersey gathering her and Jo's things.

I can't lie, I've loved having them here with me; especially Jo. He's been helping me keep my mind off shit and causing havoc in the streets. If it wasn't for him being here, I would be out hounding for Tameika, targeting anyone I thought was a connection to her. Instead, I decided to wait and let Archie do the searching while I spent as much time with Jo as I could. He was eating it up too. Jersey was a little jealous because he had been all up under me and not her. Anytime I was around, she could hang up Jo being a mama's boy. It was all about Sin.

To be real, I can't sit here and act like it's been all about Jo. Jersey and I had been getting along pretty well too. Every chance she got, she was apologizing for all the things she said and convinced me that she didn't mean any of it. I told her it was no big deal because it no longer bothered me. I could see where she was coming from, in a way. Since then, we've been getting back close, but just as friends. Nothing more.

Kacey wasn't taking Jersey living with me too well; just like I assumed. She thought I should just let Jo stay with me and Jersey stay with Amari. I couldn't do that to Jo. Separating him from his mama after a traumatic experience was the wrong thing to do. They needed each other more than anything, and I wanted my eyes on him always, until I killed Tameika myself. So, they would be living with me until then. If Kacey couldn't understand that, then she wasn't a friend.

"Where y'all going?" I asked as Jo came and stood beside me, face deep into his iPad. "Don't look at it so close, little man. You can hurt your eyes."

"Okay," he said and pulled it down some. He was watching some kids play with toys he had here. He would watch them and then mimic whatever they were doing. He was too smart for his own good.

"With me," Amari answered, emerging from the kitchen with a sandwich. "I don't want them to be alone while you are gone, so we're going back to our place."

"That's cool with me. I prefer that too. Thanks, sis."

"No biggie."

"Where you going, Sin?" Jo asked without looking up from the screen.

"I have to go handle some business with Roman. I'll be back in a little while."

"Can we play the game when you get back?" he quizzed, finally staring up at me with a shy smile; the smile he sported anytime he wanted something.

"Of course, little man," I said, and picked him up. He gave me a tight hug and I kissed his cheek before putting him down. I watched as he ran over to Jersey and sat down.

"Roman's outside waiting for you," Amari informed me with a mouthful of bread.

"Aight. I'll see y'all later."

I made it outside to find Kacey's car parked beside mine. When she noticed me, she got out and I walked over to her. I spotted Roman sitting in my car and gave him a head nod to hold on while I talked to her. I held my arms out and she walked into them, wrapping her around my torso. It had been a few days since I'd seen her face to face and I can't front, I missed her.

"What's up, Kacey?"

"Hey, Sin. Sorry to just pop up unannounced. I just wanted to see you and apologize for trippin'. I've never been in a predicament like yours and can't say how I would handle it. I was just reacting based off my feelings for you," she admitted while looking in my eyes. "I know we agreed to just be friends, but I can't deny the feelings I've grown for you. I'm not looking for us to be in a relationship or anything. I just wanted you to know."

Before I had time to process what she said, she kissed my lips and I didn't stop her. Our tongues danced and I could feel myself bricking up. This shit wasn't right, but it felt so damn good. When she moaned, I knew it was going too far. I pulled away and turned away to get myself together to end up seeing Jersey standing there with hurt and embarrassment painted on her beautiful face. Fuck! It wasn't what it looked like, but there was no need in trying to explain that to her. I had to remember that I was just friends with her and Kacey; at least, that's what I was telling myself. She broke our stare down and walked to Amari's car. I knew she was hurt, but I would have to address it later. Roman and I were already late and had to get going.

"I'm sorry," Kacey whispered.

"There's no need to apologize, Kacey. You can't help how you feel," I said, and she looked at me in shock.

"So, you don't feel the same way?"

"It's complicated. I'm not trying to run you off or avoid this conversation, but I need to go. I'm running late for a meeting," I told her. "How about we go to dinner or something later and talk about it?" I suggested to ease her mind and give me time to figure out a way to approach this bridge again. I didn't need to be distracted from my mission.

"Okay," she agreed. "See you later."

I opened her door for her as she slid inside and shut the door. I watched as she drove away before hopping in my whip and pulling off. My mind was in overdrive and I was becoming overwhelmed. I looked in the ashtray and was thankful that I had pre-rolled some tree. I put it in my mouth and fired it up, letting the smoke fill my lungs. This shit was much-needed.

"Fuck was that all about?" Roman broke the silence.

"Too much," I blew smoke.

"Y'all together?"

"Nah, nigga."

"You sure?"

"Fuck I just say?" His ass was irritating me even more.

"It was just a question, Sin. You need to calm the fuck down with all that," he barked.

"My bad, man. You know how I get when I dream about them," I sighed, taking another pull.

"That's all you had to say. You know I wouldn't be fuckin' with you if I knew."

Any time I had *that* particular dream, it would fuck up my entire mood for the day. I didn't want to be bothered by anyone. It was just how I handled shit. I didn't like talking about it, so I stayed quiet until I felt better. It could take days or weeks for me to go back to normal, and Roman respected that. He would check up on me, but keep his distance. Since we had business to tend to today, I sucked it up and decided to talk to him about it.

"You good. I should have told you. The whole situation with Kacey has me kind of fucked up."

"If it's like that, then you need to tell her what's really good. Like I always tell you, keeping shit in isn't going to help a damn thing. It only makes shit harder."

"It's not that simple, Ro. Being around Kacey brings back some haunting memories, bruh. I've been thinking about my parents a lot more lately; a lot more than I've wanted to, and I know it's because she reminds me of the past. We shared some moments together that I will never forget, and I think that's why I'm into her," I explained. "It's like, I like her, but I don't because she has an effect on me that no one will would ever understand, bruh. It's hard."

"The only thing I can tell you to do is follow your heart and figure that shit out. Yeah, that's a hard situation to be in; especially when your ass still loves Jersey, and I know living with her has made you realize that," he commented as I passed him the blunt. "She was hurt like a muthafucka seeing you suckin' Kacey's lips off her face."

"You don't think I know?" I huffed while shaking my head. "I'm not trying to be in a relationship with anyone until I figure out what the fuck I want. I'll decide once all this shit with Tameika is over with."

"Do you. Just stop holding shit in and things will be a lot easier."

I nodded my head and drove the rest of the way in silence. Five minutes later, we pulled up to Archie's place, and Tate's car was parked in the driveway. Ro and I got out and went straight inside, down to the basement. I could hear Tate griping about us being late and laughed.

"Shut up, nigga. We're here," I shouted. "What's good, Archie?"

"About damn time, man! I was about to go out and catch this bitch myself," he fumed while dapping us up.

"What you mean? You know where she at?" Roman asked the same thing I was thinking.

"Yup and if y'all late asses would have been on time, then y'all would know too."

"Stop bitchin'! We're here now. What's the word, Archie?" I asked.

"You're not going to believe this, but they've been right up under you the entire time," Archie stated. "They've been hiding out at a house that's only two doors down from yours. Which means they've been watching and keeping tabs on y'all. This bitch is a lot smarter than you think."

"You fuckin' with me, right?"

"I wish I was."

"Aye, we gotta go! I can guarantee they followed Amari to our house," Roman bet and took off up the stairs while calling Amari.

Tate and I followed behind, close on his heels. Damnit! I was underestimating this bitch. She was always a few steps ahead, but we were finally closing in on her. I just hoped that they didn't follow them, but I had a gut feeling they did.

"Baby, where y'all at?" Roman quizzed into the phone. I backed out and headed toward Roman's, driving forty over the speed limit. I couldn't let her get close to Jo again.

"Make sure all the doors are locked and the alarm is set. Get your gun, go in our bathroom with Jersey and Jo, and lock the door. Don't come out until I get there," he instructed and paused to listen to her. "Don't panic, ma. I'll be there in like ten minutes, I swear."

"Aye, tell her don't scare Jo," I whispered and he nodded his head.

The more I thought about Jo, the faster I drove. *I'm coming, son.*

4

JERSEY

I was trying to read Mari's facial expression, but it was hard. She was avoiding any eye contact with me as she talked on the phone. I watched her carefully as she grabbed her purse and went to the other room. She was hiding something, and I was going to find out what it was. I made sure Jo was okay before getting up and following behind her. I crept up behind her and remained silent as she got her gun out her purse and tucked it in her waistband. She was listening to Roman and didn't notice I was standing there until she turned around and damn near jumped out her skin. I folded my arms across my bosom and stared at her with a raised brow. She had some explaining to do.

"What's going on, Amari?"

"Nothing," she lied and started making her way around the house, checking the doors and windows. "Okay, be careful. Bushel and a peck," she said and ended the call. She then glanced at me and continued on her way, as if I wasn't going to follow her. She started turning off the lights and said, "Get Jo and follow me."

"Mari, what is going on?"

"I'll tell you in just a sec, but I need you to get Jo first and come with me," she demanded in a serious tone. "Just work with me, Jersey."

I listened to her plea and told Jo to follow us while I held his things. Amari led us to their bedroom and into their bathroom, making sure to shut and lock both doors. She grabbed some blankets from the closet and made a pallet on the floor for us to sit on, then turned the light off. I made sure Josiah was comfortable and sat down next to him as he watched his tablet.

"Start explaining," I told her.

"I can't say it out loud," she said and reverted her gaze to Jo. "I'll text it to you."

She started pecking away at her phone and I waited impatiently. I got the text and wanted to crawl under a rock after reading it. "How?"

"I'm not sure," Mari sighed. "I guess she has eyes everywhere."

I couldn't believe that Tameika had found me once again. I figured after I fucked up Vic, it would have taken her a while to get back on her mission. She was out for blood, and I knew she wasn't going to stop until I was dead.

I was about to speak when we heard car doors shut outside. Mari and I looked at one another with questionable eyes. We both got up and peeked out the window to see an unfamiliar car parked on the curb. There were two people dressed in all black walking toward the door. I squinted my eyes and my heart started racing. It was them; Tameika and Vic.

"Oh, shit, Mari. It's them."

"Fuuuccckkk!" she exclaimed. "Roman won't be here for another five minutes or so. What should we do?"

"Hide Jo and kill this bitch, that's what."

"Huh?"

"You heard me! We have to kill this bitch and her man before they get me," I whispered harshly. "Plus, I want to get her for all the pain she's caused me in my life. I won't feel better until I make her feel how I felt. Taking Jo wasn't enough."

I knew Amari probably thought I was crazy, but I was dead serious. I had been running for the past four years, and I refused to keep doing so. It was time I handled my problem head on and put an end to this shit so I could live with my son in peace.

"Okay, I'm down. Here, take this," She said, handing me her gun. "Hide Jo here in the closet and come with me while I get one of Roman's guns."

"Jo, baby. You want to play hide n seek?" I asked, and his little face lit up in excitement.

"Ooo, yes Mommy!"

"Shh," I shushed him. "Okay, listen. I need you to hide in that closet and stay in there until Mommy or Sin come to get you, understand?"

"Sin coming to play too?" he asked excitedly.

"Uh huh. Now, go hide and quietly watch your tablet. Remember, don't come out unless one of us comes to get you," I reminded him as I placed him in the closet and put a few blankets next to him. "I love you, Josiah."

"I wove (love) you too, Mommy."

I put his headphones on his ears and kissed his forehead. Closing the door, I laid my head on it and said a silent prayer over my baby as well as Amari and I. Honestly, I had no clue what I was about to walk into, but I knew it had to be done. My only prayer was that God kept us safe and alive. It would kill me if something happened to Amari, knowing she was only trying to help me fight my battle.

"You ready?" I asked, not so sure if I was myself.

"Let's go. Follow me."

We tiptoed out the bathroom and into the room. While Amari went to find the gun, I went over to the door and placed my ear up against it. I could hear whispering, which meant Tameika and Vic had made it inside the house. I silently cussed under my breath and found Amari.

"They're in here. I could hear them whispering," I whispered in her ear.

"You know how to shoot a gun, right?" she whispered back.

"No, but I'll figure it out." I assured her. "I was thinking we could stay hidden in here and make them come to us. One of us can hide in the closet and on the side of the bed. That way, when they come in, we can shoot first before they spot us," I told her the plan and she agreed. Before parting ways, she took the gun off safety and quickly showed me how to aim and shoot. Since she was a little more experienced than me in handling a gun, she laid on the side of the bed and I hid in the closet, unlocking the door first.

I tried to control my breathing as we waited for them to come in this room. At first, I was scared, but now my adrenaline was rushing through my veins. Flashbacks of the conversation I had with Tameika and how she beat my ass when I was down fueled an anger from deep inside me. This bitch had been a thorn in my side for years, and it was time to get rid of her.

I heard the room door creak open, so I peeked through the crack of the closet door and saw them creeping in. It was like I frozen in place and couldn't move. All that confidence I had a few seconds ago had disappeared. I wasn't scared. I just wasn't sure if I could pull the trigger and kill her. Was I ready to have her blood on my hands? They walked further into the room, and that's when I thought about Amari. Remembering that she was lying on the side of the bed, out in the open where they could easily find her, gave me the mojo I needed to get this shit over and done with. It was now or never. I could let them get me again, along with Amari, or get them first.

"Mommy? Can I come out? I have to pee," I heard Josiah yell from the bathroom.

"Liam!" Tameika squealed.

That was all I needed to hear. I kicked the closet door open and started firing in their direction. Out the corner of my eye, I saw Amari sit up on her knees and start shooting too. One of their bodies fell to the ground with a loud thud, but that didn't stop me from emptying the clip. By the time we were done, my ears were ringing and Josiah was screaming at the top of his lungs. Forgetting everyone and everything, I dropped the gun and ran to the bathroom. I opened the door and turned on the light to find Jo crouched down by the toilet with his hands covering his small ears. Tears and snot coated his face, and his chest was heaving up and down. When he saw me, he shot up and ran over into my arms. I kicked the door closed so he wouldn't see Tameika and Vic's lifeless bodies lying on the ground.

"Mommy, I scared!" he cried as his tiny frame quivered under my embrace. "It sound like gun."

"I'm sorry, baby. Mommy and Mari didn't mean to scare you. Everything is okay," I tried to calm him. "You don't have to be scared."

"Amari! Baby, where you at?" I heard Roman yell.

"We're in here!" she yelled back, and I heard heavy footsteps heading our way.

Picking up Jo, I sat him on the sink and grabbed a towel from the closet to clean his face. He was still a little shaken up, but he was better. It was going to eat me up inside knowing I scared him as bad as I did, but it was only to protect him. Hopefully, this didn't affect him mentally in the long run. As I was washing his face, the door opened and in walked Sincere. He closed the door and for a moment, we just stood there and stared into each other's eyes. For the first time in a while, I could read them and it made me smile.

"Sin!" Josiah shouted. He jumped down from the sink and ran to Sincere with open arms. Sincere picked him up and held him tightly with his eyes closed.

"It's okay, little man. I'm here," Sincere whispered.

"Can we go home? I don't wanna be here anymore," Jo asked as he yawned.

"We sure can. First, let me go talk to Roman. Sit in here with mommy until I come back."

"Okay."

Sincere walked over and passed Jo to me, who was fighting his sleep. We shared another intense stare down before he leaned over and kissed my forehead. The feel of his soft lips on my skin sent a shiver down my spine. It had been a while since I felt them, and I missed kissing him. Apparently, he didn't miss kissing me anymore. He had someone new and it broke my heart to see what I did earlier, but I had to shrug it off and keep it moving because I had bigger things to worry about. Now that it was all over, Sincere Peters became my biggest problem again. I stepped back, not wanting to lose control over my feelings. Salty tears burned my eyes as I thought about him kissing her. It wasn't the time to address it, so I held myself together.

He took the hint and walked away, leaving me there in my thoughts. I sat down on the toilet and let out a sigh of relief. I thanked God for allowing us to get through this safely and hoped it was the end of the storm. I was ready to be able to sit back and enjoy life without having to constantly look over my shoulder. My problems were now dead; literally. Well, my past problems were. I had a new set to deal with now, and they involved a lot of emotions I didn't want to go through.

Amari walked in and closed the door. I peeked out and saw Tameika's body being dragged across the carpet, leaving a blood trail that was sure to stain. She leaned back and let out a long, exasperated sigh.

"Bitch, you better be glad I love the hell out of you and Jo or I would not have risked me and my baby's life like that. I already know that Roman is going to be in my ass about it, but I couldn't leave you hangin'," Mari rambled, and I don't think she realized she had just spilled some major tea.

"I'm about to be a godmother?" I cheered, wiggling on the toilet seat. I wanted to get up and do a little dance, but Josiah had fallen asleep and I knew better than to wake him. He would be a mean little cranky thing, and I didn't have the energy to fuss or spank him tonight.

"Huh?" she tried to play stupid, but she was busted.

"Don't play me, cuz. I heard you loud and clear. You're about to be a mommy."

"Okay," she gave in. "Yes, I'm pregnant, but please don't tell a soul!"

"Oh my gosh! I'm so happy for you, Mari! You deserve all the happiness and more."

I was genuinely happy for my cousin. Like myself, she had been through her fair share of troubles, and I was happy to be witnessing the growth in her life. Her business was thriving, she was in love with the man of her dreams who loved her stanky draws, and she was about to experience something I would never be able to.

I hate to sound bitter, but my feelings were hurt. My ego was bruised. Tameika's harsh, but true words echoed in my ear. I never felt so low in my life. Me not being able to conceive was something I struggled with every day, but I never mentioned it and kept a smile on my face. It had always been a hard pill for me to swallow, and I never wanted to believe it. Now, it resurfaced full force like a slap in the face. It was like life was trying to force me to accept it.

"Thank you, cuz. I'm happy too, but I'm also scared," she confessed.

"Why? You have no reason to be."

"Sometimes, I just feel like it's too good to be true. Like, it's crazy how life just took us on a roller coaster ride and it seems like tonight, we finally came to the end. I don't want it to be like one of those tricky roller coasters that pauses for a few seconds and then takes a plunging dive down. I'm just ready for things to be better and stay better."

"You and me both. You just don't know how relieved I feel knowing I won't have to fear for my life anymore. Josiah and I can finally go home and let Sincere be with Kacey. I don't even want to go back there tonight, but I can manage for one more night."

"Is this about what we saw earlier?" she quizzed and leaned against the sink.

"Yeah. I'm just in my feelings, but I will get over it." I shrugged it off. I didn't want to ruin her happiness with my mixed emotions. She had dealt with enough of my problems.

"Tell him how you feel."

I looked her upside her head and rolled my eyes. "Do you not remember how that went the last time I done that? It made things worse."

"So fuckin' what? Let me tell your stubborn ass something; relationships are not easy. Not everything is supposed to be peaches and fuckin' cream, Jersey. To have growth in a relationship, you must trust, love, and communicate. You have a problem with communication and automatically give up when it's something you don't want to hear or it hurts your feelings. If you really love Sincere and don't want him to end up with Kacey, you need to sit down and get everything off your chest and listen to what he should say. If he tries to leave, don't let him. Make him talk it out with you so y'all can figure out what will be the best way to move forward from there. Show him you are willing to put in the work."

"I... I don't know how, Mari. I don't know if I can do it," I cried.

"Well, figure out before it's too late."

There was a tap at the door, and Roman stuck his head in. "Y'all okay?"

"Yes," we answered in unison.

"Cool. They just finished, so we can go now. I thought we could stay the night at the other house tonight," he told Amari.

"I'm cool with that."

Amari grabbed Jo's things for me and we left the house. Roman locked up while Sincere put Josiah in his car seat. I was so tired and ready to go to Sincere's and shower so I could cuddle up with Jo and sleep. I wanted the temporarily relief of not dealing with life's problems.

We said our byes and promised to see one another tomorrow before going our separate ways. Halfway through my silent ride with Sincere, he reached over and grabbed my hand. He pulled it to his lips and pecked it lightly, then gazed at me with a worried expression.

"You okay?"

I nodded my head yes.

"Want to talk about what happened?"

I shook my head no. "Can we talk tomorrow?"

"Only if you want to, Jay."

Jay. Maybe Mari was right. Maybe I did need to express myself, but it wouldn't be tonight. I needed at least a week to let everything sink in, then Sincere and I could have a talk I feel we had both been avoiding.

ROMAN

A few days later...

"Roman, quit!" Mari giggled. "I don't want to be late to our first app- ooohhh! Shit!" She moaned as I eased myself inside her warm, gushy opening. She had been walking around all morning in some little ass shorts and a white wife beater that had her hard nipples on display. I had been bricked up all morning and needed her assistance to help me out.

"Fuck, ma. You feel so good," I growled in her ear. Her legs were draped in the hook of my arm, and her ass was barely on the sink. She was holding onto my arms to keep her balance while digging her nails deeper into my skin with each stroke. I could feel her juices dripping down my legs; that's how wet she was. Her pussy constantly made a sloshing sound that was sending me over the edge. I slowed up my pace and went deeper inside her.

"Aaahhh," she screamed as I felt her release all over my shaft. Her grip loosened from around my arms, and her body went limp as I picked back up and came inside her.

I helped her down and started the shower. We quickly washed up and got ready to go meet with the doctor. Amari was ecstatic and couldn't wait to learn more about this experience. I was too, but I had other things on my mind that I couldn't discuss with her at this time. So, I had to try and act normal.

"I'm so anxious, Roman," she said as we were sitting in the waiting room. "I wish they would call me back."

"They will, ma. Just be patient. Didn't you say this was only an information visit or something?"

"Yeah, but it's possible they could do an ultrasound to determine how far along I am."

"How far along do you think you are?" I quizzed with a raised brow.

"Maybe six weeks."

"How many months is that?"

"One and a half."

"Why didn't you just say that?" I asked and she laughed.

"My bad," she giggled. "Weeks are what the doctors go by."

"I see I got some shit to learn," I grumbled.

I was all in on this pregnancy. This would be my first child with my future wife, and I wanted to step up and be there. I wanted to be knowledgeable on everything from the beginning to end, so I would know what to expect and how to handle it. I was going to do whatever it took to make this a smooth process for Amari. This next nine or ten months, however many it really is, was going to be dedicated to them.

"Amari White!" a nurse called out, and we followed her to an area where she checked Amari's vitals and got a urine sample.

"Will she have to do this every time?" I asked the nurse, taking notes.

"Yes, she will."

I nodded my head and let them finish. The nurse led us to an office where an older male doctor was sitting behind the desk reading over something. Aw, hell nah! Amari didn't tell me a male doctor would be all up in her pussy. I looked upside her head and she gave me a weak, guilty smile. It's cool. She better be thankful we were just sitting down to talk today, but best believe she would have a female doctor at her next visit. I don't play that shit. I'm the only nigga that gets to see her goods. Fuck outta here.

"Hello, Ms. White. I'm Dr. Gorge, it's nice to meet you," he greeted with a jolly smile. He stood up to shake her hand and then reached over to shake mine. "This must be the father."

"Yes. This is my boyfriend, Roman," Amari introduced me. I hit him with a head nod and sat down.

For the next thirty minutes, I listened and answered questions as he went over health information and background with us. I soaked in everything Amari said. This was good because I was learning more about her and vice versa. These were things we needed to know, especially for our seed.

"So, do either one of you carry the sickle cell trait?" Dr. Gorge asked.

"No."

"I do."

"What?" Amari snapped her neck to look at me and I just shrugged my shoulders.

"What?" I said back.

"Why didn't you tell me?" She pondered with a hint of fear in her eyes.

"I just never thought it was a big deal," I answered honestly. "It's not like I have it; it's just the trait."

"That can play a big role on whether the baby has it," Dr. Gorge informed us, and I was surprised.

"It can?"

"Yes. Since you carry the trait, you can pass it on to the baby and that could possibly lead to him or her having the actual disease," he explained, and my mind was blown.

I knew that sickle cell was more common in African Americans than any other race, but I never thought just because I had the trait that I could pass it to my kids. I glanced at Amari, who was evidently worried. Her face was scrunched up and she was pulling at her pouty bottom lip. Reaching over, I grabbed her hand and gave her a reassuring smile.

"How high is the possibility? I asked.

"It's about 50/50. We won't know until the baby is born, but even then, it might not show up right away. It's a waiting game. Any more questions?"

"No, thank you," Amari spoke up.

"Would you like to see the baby and hear his or her heartbeat? I want to get the exact due date for you and see how far along you are," he suggested, and that changed Amari's somber mood. She eagerly agreed with a smile tugging at her lips. We were escorted to another room where an ultrasound technician was waiting for us. Amari hopped on the table while I took a seat in front of the 32" TV.

"How are y'all today? And congratulations to the both of you," the technician greeted with a smile.

"Thank you," Amari and I answered in unison and smiled at one another.

"Okay, mom. I need you to lift your shirt a little so I can put this paper protection around your waist, and then I'll squirt this warm gel on your stomach so we can see and hear the baby," the nurse explained, and Amari obeyed.

"How often will she get an ultrasound?" I questioned as I watched her prep Mari. I was dead ass when I said I was all in and wanted to know everything. I was going to be the dad they kicked out the room for asking too many questions and being up under them, inspecting. I still found it hard to believe I was going to be a father, but I already loved my seed more than anything and would go above and beyond to make sure Rome was good.

"Not often, unless the doctor feels it is needed," she explained as she rubbed something across Mari's stomach. "There goes baby! It looks like you're about seven weeks along, which means you will due July 25th. A summer baby!"

"Oh, I heard being pregnant in the summer was the worst," Mari complained with a frown. "I don't want to be big and miserable."

"I'll be there to make sure you won't be miserable, but I can't do anything about you being big. Rome is going to blow your ass up," I joked, and she stuck her tongue out at me.

"No, *she* won't."

"Uh oh. I already see there's going to be a fight over the gender," the nurse giggled. "Let's listen to the heartbeat and then you'll be good to go."

Thump. Thump. Thump.

Hearing my seed's heartbeat so loud and steady for the first time brought tears to my eyes. This was only the first appointment and I already couldn't wait for him to be here. I couldn't wait to hold him in my arms and watch him grow up. I was going to make sure he didn't turn to the streets like me. All the businesses and shit I had would be going in his name the day he was born. Rome was going to be set before he was even born. Getting up, I walked over to Amari and wiped the tears from her eyes, then kissed her lips. She gazed up at me with those loving green eyes and smiled.

"I can't believe we're going to be parents," she sighed. "I wouldn't want it to be with anyone else."

"Likewise, ma. Bushel and a peck."

"Hug around the neck."

~&~

I was thankful to be the only one on the elevator. I was at UAB visiting Ken, but also to ask him and Julian for Amari's hand in marriage. I was nervous as fuck because I didn't know what to expect from either one of them, but it was something I wanted to do. Other than Ma, their opinions mattered the most, and it would mean a lot to Amari for me to ask them both. That is, when she found out. I wasn't worried about A'Marie because she had welcomed me into the family since day one. She would be overjoyed for her one and only daughter to be getting married.

The elevator chimed and the doors open. The overbearing hospital smell greeted me and tore my stomach the fuck up. I'd always hated the smell of them, but today it seemed to be damn near unbearable. Covering my nose with my shirt, I stepped off and speed-walked to Ken's room. I knocked twice and then walked in to find Ken and Julian talking.

"What's up, y'all," I greeted them.

"What's up, Roman. Where's Mari?" Kendrick quizzed as I dapped Julian up and he pulled me in for a hug.

"She doesn't know I'm here," I admitted, and they both looked at me funny. I pulled a chair up and sat down so I was facing them both.

"I'm surprised. You sure that's a good thing?" Julian joked, and we all laughed. "I just know how my daughter can be."

"Because you got her that way, Dad," Ken stated the obvious. It was no secret that Amari was a daddy's girl.

"Yeah, I know," Julian agreed. "So, what do you need to talk to us about, Roman? Even though I think I already have a clue."

"Yeah, me too," Ken cosigned, so I decided to see what they were thinking.

"What y'all think it is?"

They looked at one another with matching smirks. Hell, matching everything. It was crazy how much Ken looked like Julian. He should have been a junior.

"Nah, I want to hear what you have to say first, and then I'll tell you," Julian challenged.

"I want to propose to Amari, and I wanted permission from the both of you first," I spoke confidently, but on the inside, I was shaking with anticipation. I rubbed my palms over my pants and leaned back. My phone was vibrating in my pocket, but I ignored it. I could call whoever it was back.

"Why do you want to marry my daughter?" Julian interrogated as he leaned forward with his elbows on his knees, looking me in the eyes.

"I love Amari more than anything in this world. She's complete me in more ways than one, and I can't imagine my life without her. I know it's only been a few months, but my feelings for her are true. I want to be the man that keeps her happy. I want her to know that I will be more than a husband to her. I will be her best friend, her soulmate, her protector; all that and so much more. I'm not too good at expressing myself, but all I can say is that I love your daughter and don't want to go on without us sharing the same last name. I've never wanted something more in my life."

Julian put me on the spot and I know what I said probably sounded cliché, but it was all the truth. No one would ever understand how I felt about Amari because they weren't me, and they didn't know the woman that I knew. The caring, loving and understanding woman that I had grown to love more and more every day. If I didn't get their blessing, then we were eloping. Real shit. We would hop on my jet and go to a private island. I already had her ring, so it wouldn't be a problem. That's how bad I wanted to marry her, and I refused to let anyone get in my way.

"You're good for my sister, Roman. I can see that now because at first, I didn't. I was just going off what I had heard about you. I was judging you before I got to know you, and I apologize for that. Mari had already been through so much with that nigga, Nigel, that I didn't want her to end up in the same predicament or worse. I'm glad you proved me wrong. I'm cool with you coming into the family," Kendrick expressed and I can't lie, it had a nigga feeling good as hell.

I wasn't surprised that he judged me from the start; who doesn't? I can admit that some of the things he probably heard about me were true. I'd done some fucked up shit in my life, but it was all by choice. No one forced me to do those things, and no one could. I was my own person, and I had control over my life. Still, none of that defined me. I was raised up right, and it stuck with me. Just because I created new habits didn't mean the old habits instilled in me had gone.

"I appreciated that, bruh." I thanked him and then looked at Julian, who had yet to speak. He was now sitting back with his ankle on his knee. His face was blank; expressionless. The fuck did that mean? I would hate for this nigga to tell me no and then try to fuck me up after finding out I was his son-in-law. My mind was set; I was marrying Amari.

"Dad?" Kendrick broke the silence.

"What, son?"

"Are you going to answer him?"

Yeah, nigga. Are you going to answer me?

Julian sighed heavily and rubbed his hands across his face before glaring at me with those creepy ass eyes. Amari's did that shit too when her moods changed. They would be a sparkling emerald one minute, and a glowing hazel the next. It was sexy and creepy all at the same time.

"You have my blessing as well, but if you so much as hurt a hair follicle on her head, I was kill you. And it won't be quick and easy. I will make you suffer until I feel you've had enough. That could be a few days or a few years. Now, I like you, Roman. Like Kendrick said, you're good for Amari. You bring out something in her we haven't seen in a long time. I love seeing her like that, and I'm depending on you to keep it that way."

The smile that tugged at my lips was probably a mile long. A nigga was so happy. It felt good to know that both Ken and Julian accepted me. With Amari being the only girl, I knew they were the two I would have to worry about. Not anymore.

I stayed for a while longer, catching up and learning new things about Amari. Before I left, I told them my proposal plan and showed them the ring. Julian thought it would be best if I left the ring with him so Amari wouldn't find it. I promised to get up with them later and left to go home to my future wife.

HARMONY

It had been two days since I was released from the hospital, and I felt I had enough energy to get up and get shit done today. The investigator had been blowing my phone up to get my statement. While I was in the hospital, I told them I didn't want any visitors and would never say a word while the investigator was there. I wasn't ready to talk. I wasn't ready to relive what was already playing through my head almost every second of the day. Thoughts of that night were starting to consume me, and I felt myself slipping into a depression that I fought to stay out of. I'd dealt with depression firsthand, and I never want to experience it again.

"Hey, best. You okay?" Fancy asked as she came and sat next to me on the bed. I had been at her place since the doctor suggested that someone stay with me for at least a week. She welcomed me with open arms and had been helping me out. I was thankful.

"Yeah, just thinking."

"About Detrix?" she joked, and I wanted to slap her.

Detrix had played me. He was a pussy. The day I was released from the hospital, I got Fancy to drive by the hotel we were at to see if his car was there. I thought he would have stayed and tried to find me, but nope. His ass got the hell out of Birmingham. I called him from Fancy's phone and when he heard my voice, he hung up and blocked the number. I know because I tried to call numerous times. I mean, damn. He could have at least called the police or something.

"No, bitch. Don't mention that name around me."

"My bad," she giggled. "Tell me what you're thinking about and I won't be guessing the wrong thing."

"Have you heard anything else about Kendrick?" I asked as I stared at the ceiling.

I missed him and wanted to go see him, but I wasn't taking that chance. When I was in the hospital and one of the nurses informed me that Amari was there to see me, I knew it wouldn't be a pleasant visit. I would probably be dead instead of talking to Fancy if I had allowed her to come back. I'm pretty sure she found out about all the grimy shit I did with the help of Tiffani, and more than likely, she had come to see me to get revenge. I quickly denied and asked to be moved. The thought of running into her was what kept me from going to see Kendrick. That, and I was also scared to face him. I was scared to look him in the eyes while knowing I was the reason for his predicament.

"No, and even if I did, I wouldn't tell you," she answered in an annoyed tone.

"And why not?"

"Because, Harm. You need to go see him and find out for yourself."

"You know I can't do that," I argued.

"And why not?" She mimicked me, and it almost made me smile. Almost.

"It's all my fault," I whimpered. "If it wasn't for my sneaking around, Warren never would have shot him. If I would have just stayed and not ran to Mobile to get away from my problems, then it wouldn't have happened. If it wasn't for me, it never would have happened."

"You have to stop doing that," Fancy sighed while massaging her temples. "Yes, you played a part in the way it transpired, but it's not your fault. You didn't pull the trigger, Warren did. Stop taking the blame for what someone else did and just own up to your faults. You are not responsible for it, Harmony."

I loved Fancy and the fact that she was trying to make me feel better, but the shit she was saying was going in one ear and out the other. No one could tell me otherwise. When you broke down the root of the problem, all fingers pointed back at me. That made me solely responsible for all the shit that went down. That's how I saw it, and I'm pretty sure everyone else did too.

"Whatever," I mumbled and carefully stood to my feet. "Are you still going to take me down to the precinct so I can talk to this annoying ass man?" I asked to remind her, and to change the subject.

"You know I am. I thought that afterward, we could go grab a bite to eat. You haven't been out the house, and you could use some fresh air," she suggested and for a moment, that didn't sound like a bad idea. Then, I remembered that my face was still a little fucked up and I didn't want anyone to see me like this. Thankfully, it was still cold and I could wear a scarf to cover up some of it.

"I'm not ready to go out like that yet, Fancy. I want my face to heal more," I explained while putting on my shoes.

"It doesn't look as bad as you think it does. Ain't that right, baby?" she yelled to Z, who had just walked in the door. He came to the back room that I was occupying and grabbed Fancy by the waist and kissed her neck. I looked away to brush off the twinge of jealousy that was trying to invade my veins. I remembered when Kendrick would do that to me. It would have me hot and ready like Little Caesars. I missed the little things, but I had to go and fuck things up.

"What y'all talking about?" Z asked.

"I want to take her out to lunch, but she doesn't want to because of her face," Fancy explained to him. "I told her it doesn't look as bad as she thinks."

Z looked at me and back at Fancy with a straight face. "Don't be lying to your friend, baby. Her shit is still fucked up."

"Zion!" Fancy squealed and shoved him a little. That's when his tight lips broke into a smile and he laughed.

"I'm just fuckin' with you, Harmony. You good, ma. Go look in the bathroom."

I went to the bathroom and saw that they were right. My face was healing well, but not enough for me to be comfortable out in public. Both of my eyes were still a little black and my left one was slightly swollen. I had two staples in the middle of my forehead and a cut on my jaw. My bottom lip was bruised, but the swelling had gone down. Warren had done a number on me, but I was just thankful to be alive. At one point, I just knew I was going to die. God spared me.

"Come on, Harmony. Z heated the car up before he came in," Fancy yelled. How was she now the one rushing me?

Fifteen minutes later, we arrived at the precinct and I was ready to leave. I didn't feel like going in here and explaining my story, but it had to be done. Fancy offered to come with me, but I declined and told her to just wait in the car. Pulling the scarf around my face tighter, I battled the cold, harsh November winds to the steps and inside.

"I'm here to see Detective Cunnings," I informed the front desk clerk when I heard footsteps creep up behind me. I turned around and was met with a big, burly guy with a cup of coffee in his hands and a smile.

"Ms. Knight. I've been waiting for you. Please, come with me," he said and turned to walk away. Hesitantly, I followed him until we made it to an office. "Have a seat," he offered one of the chairs sitting in front of his desk.

I took a seat and observed his office. It was bland with no color. There were no pictures of him or family. The only thing that stood out was the calendar with the daily devotion on it. *Please, don't let this be long.*

"So, Ms. Knight. This should be quick and simple. All I need you to do is write out your statement so I can have it on file and you are free to go," he stated, and it was like music to my ears.

"Is that all?" I had to ask to be sure. I didn't need any surprises.

"Yes. We have all the evidence we need to close out this case. You were the victim and you had to defend yourself to save your life. Simple."

I nodded my head and fought back the tears as he handed me paper and pen. It took me a while, but I finished without leaving out one single detail from that night. I wanted them to know how much of a monster Warren was, and why I had no choice but to kill him. I know it sounds harsh, but I was happy I did. I thanked Detective Cunnings and left with the weight of the world lifted from my shoulders. It was like all that sadness and baggage was removed and I could breathe easier. It was a good feeling.

"What happened?" Fancy asked as I opened the door.

"Damn, girl. Let me get in," I chuckled, then winced in pain as I eased into the seat. My body was letting me know I had been doing too much and needed to slow down.

"You okay?"

"Yeah, just hurting a little."

"So? What happened?"

"Nothing. I went in there and wrote out my statement. Now, I'm here."

"That's all?"

"That's the same thing I asked," I giggled. "Yup. He said they had all the evidence they need, and it was clear that I was the victim."

"Which is true. I'm glad that's one less thing you have to worry about, best."

"Me too," I agreed.

She leaned over and gave me a hug before pulling off into traffic. I laid my head back and was about to close my eyes when I noticed her take the wrong exit on purpose. I looked at her and she was tapping away at her steering wheel, trying to evade my glare.

"Fancy?"

"Huh?"

"Where are you going?"

"Home, why?" She played dumb.

"Bitch, no you ain't. This isn't the way to the projects," I snapped and she laughed.

"Don't say it like that! It's cool because Z and I are moving soon anyway," she boasted.

"And?"

"And?" she repeated with a deep scowl and finally looked at me. "What you mean and? You're not happy for your friend?"

"Yes, I am, but that doesn't have shit to do with where you're going."

"Okay," she breathed in defeat. "I'm taking you to the hospital, Harm. You're going to see Kendrick."

"Oh, no the hell I'm not! Turn around right now, Fancy!" I demanded.

"Or what?" she challenged. "This is something you *need* to do, Harm! You can't avoid it forever. He's the father of your kids, so you would end up doing it anyway. Why not now?"

Why did she have to make a good point? Yes, I needed to speak with Kendrick, but what was I going to say? Better yet, would he want to listen? There was a lot to consider going into this situation, but Fancy wouldn't understand that. No one would. I wanted to protest, but decided against it. If I wanted to move forward, then this was something I had to do. I just prayed Amari wasn't there.

"Okay," I gave in. "Just don't leave me."

"Bet."

We rode to the hospital in silence. Fancy found a parking spot close to the door and walked me to it. My knees buckled and I wanted to change my mind, but it was too late. I was already here, so why not go ahead and get it over with?

"I'm so scared, Fancy. What if everything goes wrong?" I cried in panic. "I've done so much wrong that there's no way I can make things right."

"Stop it! Stop thinking negatively. You won't know until you try, now go. You got this, bestie," she encouraged and embraced me tightly.

"I don't know what I would do without you."

She let me go and promised to be waiting for me in the car. I took a deep breath and went inside to face the love of my life for the first time in weeks.

5

KENDRICK

My eyes were growing heavy, and I was ready for a nap when there was a light knock at my door. It was so low that I had to wait for them to knock again to make sure I wasn't hearing things. I wasn't expecting any visitors. Anyone that normally came to see me knew I wanted to get some rest, so I had no idea who it could be. I had the right mind to just ignore them and go to sleep, but I was curious.

"Come in!" I yelled and the door slowly opened, revealing the last person I thought I would see. Harmony. What was she doing here, and how did she know where I was? She had refused Amari's visits, but wanted to come see me. I wasn't in the right state of mind for any bullshit she wanted to pull today.

"Hey," she whispered shyly. She stood over by the door with her hands folded in front of her.

She had a scarf covering half her face, but I could still see what she was trying to hide. The cuts and bruises were somewhat fresh, which means this happened recently. And I bet I know exactly who did it. As I observed her, I couldn't figure out whether I felt sorry for her or just didn't give a fuck. She was the one who put herself in this situation. That doesn't mean he should have done her like that. No man should ever put his hands on a woman. Maybe yoke her up a little bit, but not straight up beat her like she's another man. He was that type of grimy person; had to shoot me because he couldn't fight, so this was expected out of him.

"What are you doing here?" I asked while grilling her.

Her being in my presence was upsetting me because all I could think about was I wouldn't be here if it wasn't for her. If she could have remained faithful or shit, even told me she wasn't feeling me anymore, none of this would have happened. If she could have just loved me like I loved her.

"I... uhm... I heard about what happened and I wanted to come... to come see you," she stammered while shifting her weight.

"For what?" I spat and she took a step back with shock written all over her face.

"To make sure you were okay, Ken."

"Okay, you see that I am. Now, you can leave."

"That's not all."

"What else?"

"I wanted to apologize. I mean, I am apologizing. I'm sorry, Kendrick. I'm sorry for hurting you and doing all the scandalous shit I done; for the lies, the cheating, the selfishness. I'm so sorry. You did nothing to deserve any of it. You were the perfect man who treated me like a queen, but I was too selfish and greedy to appreciate you. I was stupid for making those choices, and I realize that now. I know it may be too late, but can you find it in your heart to please forgive me?" She cried. Her words didn't move me. I was glad she apologized, but the only reason she did was because things didn't go as she planned.

"Now, you want to apologize. Why? Because things didn't go as you thought they would?" I interrogated with a raised brow. "Tell me, if Warren didn't beat the fuck out of you, would you have even cared?"

"Of course, I would have! I've never stopped caring," she gasped as if she was offended. The nerve of her.

"Don't try to feed me that bullshit, Harmony! If you cared, you never would have done any of that shit!" I yelled a little louder than I intended. Feelings I forgot I had were starting to resurface. For so long, I had been so angry and hurt by Harmony that I intentionally made myself bury them so I could move on. Guess you never get over something until you addressed it and got closure. That's what I needed, so I wasn't going to hold back on her.

"That's not fair, you can't say that."

"Why can't I? You know what, there's been a lot that I haven't said that I should have a long time ago. Harmony, you hurt me. You tore me down and bruised my ego as a man, lover and provider. At first, I thought it was something that I was doing. I did my best to love you. I spoiled you with time, sex, and attention! I made sure you were straight before myself because that's what a man is supposed to do. You were too ungrateful to realize that. Yeah, I did have my seasons where I worked a lot, but no matter how many hours of the day I worked, I would come home and spend it with you. At least, I would try because half the time, you would be out with Fancy, or so I thought. You were out there fuckin' my best friend behind my back!" I barked, causing her to jump. "Why him, Harm? Out of all the gotdamn people in the world, you choose to screw him? The one nigga you knew I considered to be my brother. Not only did you fuck up our relationship, but mine with him as well."

She was bawling her eyes out while I laid there feeling better than when she first came in. I needed to do that and she needed to hear it. I loved her and I still do, but her coming in here with a weak ass apology wasn't going to solve anything or change how I felt about her. She was dead to me. Keyana and Hayden were the only reasons I would have anything to do with her. If it wasn't for them, she would no longer be in my life.

"I know that, Kendrick, and all I can do is apologize and show you how truly sorry I am. I... I know you won't forgive me right away, but at least think about it. I miss you," she had the audacity to slip in.

"I'm not Warren."

"He's dead," she mumbled, but I heard her loud and clear.

"He's dead?"

"Yes."

Damn. I couldn't believe it and to be real, I didn't know how to feel about it. Before all the bullshit, Warren was my right hand. Just like I still loved Harmony, I still loved him too. He was family at one time, and knowing he was gone fucked with me. He left me with some unanswered questions that only he could answer.

"How? What happened?" I pondered, shaking my head in disbelief.

"I... I did it. I killed him," she confessed and broke down once again. "I didn't mean to do it, but I had to save myself. He had already killed my baby, and I couldn't let him kill me."

Without warning, she walked over and sat on the edge of the bed. Still sobbing, she went on to tell me everything that she had been through with Warren. The shit was fucked up and no one should ever have to endure the things that she did. She may have done her own dirt, but that didn't mean she deserved being repeatedly raped and beaten. All because he wanted to get back at me. When she said that, I had to clear my ears and get her to say it again. I looked in her eyes as she talked and knew she wasn't lying about any of it. I can honestly say that I felt bad for her.

"Damn," I breathed. "You didn't deserve that."

"Yes, I did." She sniffled. "Look at all the shit I done. All that was just karma coming back to bite me in the ass."

"Nah, that was Warren being a pussy ass nigga. Don't take the blame for what he did. You were abused in the worst possible way. You were violated, Harmony. Don't feel bad for protecting yourself. I'd rather you done that than leave our kids motherless. They miss you."

"I miss them too, so much. I should have never left."

"Why did you leave?" I asked.

"I was trying to run away from my problems. I thought that if I left for a year or two and let things die down, then I would have no worries when I came back," she explained. "I figured over time, you would somehow forgive me and Warren would have forgotten about me."

Sighing heavily, I closed my eyes and tried to figure out why I suddenly felt like I could forgive her. I knew it was because I sympathized with her and wanted to work on being cordial for the kids. Now that she was back, I needed her to be more active in Keyana and Hayden's lives. Since I've been up and they knew she was here, they've been asking everyone about her and why she hadn't come to get them. I didn't want that for them. So, if that meant forgiving Harmony, then that's what I would do; day by day. She had a lot to prove before I completely accepted that she was a different person.

"Look, Harm. I'm going to be honest; I'm not going to forgive you over night. Heartbreak takes time to heal, but our situation is a little different because we have kids involved. You must stop being selfish and put them first. They know you're around and they've been asking why you haven't come to see them. See how stupid decisions can distract you from what's important in your life? Those kids need you; they need us. Off the strength of them, I'm willing to try and put all this shit behind us."

The expression on her face was priceless as she stared at me in disbelief. She was speechless. She just kept moving her mouth, but nothing would come out. Like I knew she would, she started crying again.

"Th... thank you so much, Kendrick. I... am so sorry."

"Thank God instead," I told her. This conversation with her had drained me and I was getting tired again. I yawned to throw a hint. I wanted to sleep in peace.

"Are you tired?" she quizzed.

"Yeah. I was almost asleep when you came."

"Oh, I'm sorry. Would you like for me to leave?"

"It's up to you," I yawned again.

"Do you mind if I stay?" she asked what I hoped she wouldn't. "I'm staying with Fancy and I don't want to overstay my welcome. Her and Z are in a good place, and I don't want to ruin it by being there. I will leave when visiting hours are over."

I sighed deeply and contemplated on my answer. Since I'd woken up, shit had been moving too fast for me. With the head injuries I suffered, I constantly had a migraine and would forget some shit. Dr. Kennings said it was normal for an injury like mine, and she was working on something just for me. Low key, she was feeling a young, paralyzed nigga. These eyes got her every time. Nah, let me stop. I had other things to think about.

"I don't know if that's a good idea, Harmony. Shit is too fresh and if my parents or Amari come, all hell will break loose."

"That's the thing, I want them to see me. I know it isn't going to be pretty, but I need to apologize to them too. I know that not only did I hurt you, but I hurt them as well; especially A'Marie. She expected more from me," she stated with a somber look on her bruised face. Despite all that, she was still beautiful to me. Looking at her and reminiscing on all that we've been through, I was surprised that we were sitting here being cordial with one another. Honestly, it would be different if I weren't paralyzed. I would have choked her ass out again for leaving our kids, but that was in the past now and I was praying that our future as friends and parents would be a lot better.

"Are you sure you're up for that?" I quizzed, feeling myself dozing off. "It's not going to be all peaches and cream right away. Like myself, they will still have some animosity toward you until they can fully forgive you and move on."

"Yes, I know that. I'm just trying to be a better person and it starts off with family, right? I'm a changed person, Ken. I know it's going to take time for me to prove myself, but I'm willing to do whatever to do so."

"I hear you. Actions speak louder than words, so we will see."

"So, is that a yes?" she asked, and I opened my eyes to look at her.

"Yes, you can stay. I'm going to sleep, now. The pain meds are kickin' in," I said groggily and closed my eyes again.

"Thank you, Ken," she whispered and kissed my forehead. That's all I remember before sleep consumed me.

AMARI

It was hard keeping my pregnancy secret. I was so overjoyed and wanted to tell my mama more than anyone, but decided I would just keep my word and tell everyone at my grand opening. I had already slipped and told Jersey; I didn't want to do the same thing again. Speaking of my grand opening, it was only a few weeks away and I had so much to do. Lola had called and got in my ass about it and demanded we go start working tomorrow. I had been procrastinating, mainly because this fatigue was kickin' my ass. It was hard for me to find the energy to do anything but go see Kendrick, which I was doing now.

Visiting hours would be over soon, so I was in a rush. I had the urge to see him, so I told Roman where I was going and he just rolled over and went back to sleep. It was so cute how he was experiencing some of the same symptoms I was. He was always complaining about being sleepy all the time and how much he had been eating. Since then, he was getting up faithfully and going to the gym. He said he refused to gain baby weight with me. I would make sure he gained a few pounds, and I'm not talking about in muscle either.

Lately, the thought of Roman carrying the sickle cell trait was in the back of my mind. I didn't want to think negatively, but I couldn't help it. I was scared that my baby would have sickle cell. That wasn't something I wouldn't be able to handle, so I prayed God heard my cry and covered my unborn.

I made it to the hospital and threw my car in park. I jogged to the entrance and elevators. Kendrick was probably asleep, but he was going to wake up for me. He could go back to sleep once I left. Those pain meds have him on cloud nine, so I know his high ass be sleeping good.

I did my signature knock and opened the door to only become enraged. I was livid. This bitch was sitting here sleep, all comfortable like I wasn't about to fuck her ass up. The fuck was she doing here, anyway?

"Why are you here, bitch?" I yelled with my arms folded, startling them both. Harmony's eyes bucked when they landed on me, and I heard Ken let out a loud sigh.

"Mari, don't do this, please. My head is pounding and you just scared the shit out of me," Ken said in an annoyed tone. Hearing that he had a migraine made me step away and calm down a little. I didn't want to make anything worse when he was making so much progress. He better be glad I loved him because this shit was hard as hell. It was taking everything in me not to go over there and pounce on her big ass. I spun around on my toes to face Ken. There was no telling what I might do if I laid eyes on her again.

"Can you please tell me what is going on?" I demanded through gritted teeth. "My palms are itchin' to slap a bitch, and the urge just keeps getting stronger," I said loud enough for her to hear. My hands were on my hips and I was tapping my foot against the glossy tile floor. *Wait until I tell Mama about this.*

"Everything is good, Amari. She's good, I'm good; we're good, and I need y'all to be too," he explained, and I wanted to slap his dumb ass back into a coma. Was he serious?

"You have got to be kiddin' me, Kendrick?"

"I'm not."

"And why in the flyin' fuck do you think I would forgive *that* bitch?" I growled while shoving my finger in Harmony's direction.

When he closed his eyes, I felt bad because I was letting my temper get the best of me. He knew how I was, so he was trying to be patient with me. *Let me try this again.* "I mean, why do you feel we need to be good? She's dead to me; I'm done."

"She's the mother of your niece and nephew, Mari."

"And? The fu- why does that matter to me? And why does it matter to you? What they put in your IV, Ken? Do I need to call the nurse, because you're a bit delusional?"

"You know why it matters to me," he implied. "Just hear her out, sis. It was hard for me too at first, but I couldn't just shut her out. I'm not saying that I've just forgiven her for everything and swept it under the rug because that's far from the truth. I'm doing this for Keyana and Hayden, so will you do it for me?" he pleaded with big puppy dog eyes, but that didn't work. I was unmoved; unbothered. The only thing I wanted from that bitch was for her to kiss my fat ass. Fuck. Harmony.

"Nope. Eh eh. Not gon' happen," I denied, imitating New New from *ATL*. He tried to hide the smirk that tugged at the creases of his lips, but I saw that. He loved when I did that because he would say I sounded just like her. I guess he was trying to be serious for the unwanted guest in the room.

"Come on, Mari."

"No, Kendrick. It's fine. I think I'll just leave," Harmony mumbled and I shrugged my shoulders, then sat down in the chair. Bye, hoe. Be gone.

"You're not leaving, Harmony and Amari, you're going to listen to what she has to say," he barked, like that would phase me. He may look like him, but he was not Julian White and I was grown as fuck. I was doing them a favor by ignoring her and addressing him. UAB hospital would be on lockdown, and Roman would be bailing me out of jail.

"It's fine, really. You can't force her to do anything she doesn't want," she replied and I was a little stunned. This didn't sound like the old Harmony. The old Harmony would have started yappin' that trap the first time I called her a bitch. She had let it slide by not one, but three times. She had Ken fooled, but not me. This was all an act to get back in good graces with everyone for her to turn around and do some more grimy shit, which would result in an ass whoopin'.

"You damn straight," I cosigned.

"Come sit down next to her," Kendrick said to her. I whipped my neck around and mugged his ass.

"Who come sit down where?"

"You heard me, Mari. Y'all are going to talk; you can't avoid it. I'd rather this happen now than later. Plus, I think this will help my progress. I won't be stressed and worried about any of this anymore. My mind will be clear, and I can fully focus on getting better," he explained and I wanted to roll over and die. The love I had for my brother made me agree. If he honestly thought me listening to her would be beneficial to his mental health, then I was all for it. I would do anything for him and he knew it. He knew exactly what to say to get me to agree.

"Make it quick. Visiting hours are almost over," I said to Harmony and damn near jumped out my seat when I looked at her. Her face was all types of fucked up, but it looked like it was healing some. There was a twinge of sympathy poking at my heart for her. She looked broken, and I knew that feeling all too well. Oh well. She did that to herself.

She quickly sat down and faced me. Tears were on the verge of spilling over as she took a deep, shaky breath. I could tell that she was nervous, and she should have been. All I had to do was reach over and pop her in her chest. Her face already had enough damage.

"Amari, I would like to apologize for all the chaos I've caused, not only in Kendrick's life, but yours as well. I was just so angry and jealous of you. Jealous of the relationship that you had with Ken and how he cherished you. I've never had that with any of my siblings. I don't even talk to my family, so why I went and messed up with the closest thing I had to family? I don't know. I was stupid, selfish. I was fighting with some inner demons and taking it out on the wrong people. The only people who loved me. I know you've never really cared for me, but at one point, you accepted me. I want us to get back to that and then grow from there. I'm not asking that you forgive me immediately, but I'm asking that you at least consider it. The shit I've been through because of my own stupid decisions has opened my eyes. It's made me realize how much of a monster I was, and for what? I was so blessed and didn't see it because I was too busy worried about what I didn't have, or what I could have. I had more than some could say they've ever had. All I'm saying is that I'm truly sorry from the bottom of my heart, and I pray you find it in your heart to forgive me one day. Bye, y'all."

With tears staining her bruised face, she quickly walked over and kissed Ken on his forehead before zooming out the room. She didn't give me a chance to respond; probably because she feared my response. I was thankful that she did because this gave me some time to let her words soak in and not just react without thinking. I had trouble with that and made a mental note to work on it.

"You don't have to forgive her now, and we don't have to walk about it. Just think it over and go from there. I hope your mean, stubborn and spoiled ass can forgive her and move on. If I can, anyone should be able to. She hurt me more than anybody," Kendrick expressed as I stared off into space. "Now, call the nurse and tell her to bring me something for this migraine."

Oh yeah. I could hear some of the old Ken in that."

~&~

"Pop that pussy, bitch!" Lola sang loudly along with Rick Ross, poppin' in my passenger seat. I just shook my head and laughed as he swung the 22-inch wig he had bought on a dare, but he was feelin' himself now. "Ooo, Ms. Mari, you shouldn't have ever taken me in that wig store, hunny; got a girl feelin' herself."

"That was a mistake," I chuckled. "You're doing too much over there in that seat," I joked as I turned into the *Galleria* parking lot and searched for a parking spot. I was salty Lola chose this mall because it stayed packed and I didn't feel like being around people today. My hormones were all over the place and I couldn't control them. I was so moody and I hated it. I hoped it was just a phase because it could affect my business if I couldn't control them.

"Whatever, girl. You're just hating," he teased with a wink. "Oh, my gahd! Watch where the fuck you're goingggg!" He rolled down the window and screamed at the car in front of us. They were coming down the aisle the wrong way and had the nerve to honk at us. They shot him a bird and I had to hurry and roll up his window; I placed it on child lock before he could touch the button.

"Let it go, boo. Let it go. It's not that deep," I stated as I waited for a car to back out a front parking spot. I wasn't about to pass that up.

"Yes, it is! I'm in this car, Mari! What if they would have hit us and scratched up my face or something? I don't need an ugly scar on this pretty face," he dramatically expressed while looking in the mirror. I ignored his conceited ass and killed the engine. I stepped out the car, looking good as ever. It had been a while since I dressed up and I felt this was the perfect occasion, especially since Lola was always dressed to kill.

My hair was straightened and curled into some big spirals. I had on minimal makeup, but enough to enhance my beauty and bring out the hazel specs that were scattered throughout my green eyes. I had on some dark blue ripped jeans that had the rips right under my ass cheeks, but not enough to show. My olive-colored loose-fitting, off the shoulder shirt went great with my wheat Timberland heels.

"Let's stop at the food court first, I'm hungry," I suggested as we crossed the walkway.

"We just ate two hours ago! You must be about to come on or something; over there sounding like hungry, hungry hippo. Come on, girl."

"Speaking of hippos, she's resurfaced."

"Who?"

"Harmony," I spat and rolled my eyes.

"No the fuck she didn't, bitch! Where you see her sneaky, runaway love ass at?" he fumed, and I had to stop walking from laughing at how serious he was.

"Runaway love?" I managed to ask between laughs.

"You know that old ass song."

"Yeah, but she was at the hospital with Ken when I went to see him yesterday."

"He knew?" he asked, shocked.

"Yeah. He demanded that I sat down and heard what she had to say, so I did. She apologized and explained to me why she done the things she did. I can understand, in a way. I just wish she would have handled it differently and maybe things would have turned out different."

"You forgive her?"

"I don't know. It's going to take me a while to figure out," I admitted. Deep in my heart, I knew it was the right thing to do, but it was easier said than done. The damage was done and it would take a while to fix it. "Oh, and I never told you that she was the also responsible for the shop burning down."

"The fuck you just say, Mari?"

"You heard me. I found out because Roman paid Tiffani a visit after finding out it was her and she spilled the tea, pipin' hot for you."

"You better not forgive her triflin', hatin' ass! How about we set her big ass on fire and see how she likes it," he ranted while stomping ahead of me.

Lola went to get some ice cream while I ordered Chinese. I was waiting to place my order when someone caught my eyes. They looked different, but I was sure it was them. I discreetly watched as they went to order some food as I got mine. I went to the table Lola had chosen for us and sat down with my eyes still glued on them. Of course, Lola's nosey ass peeped game and followed my gaze. When he noticed who it was, he set his ice cream down and jumped up from his seat.

"I've been waitin' to see this bitch," he yelled back as he ran full speed and tackled Tiffani. I watched in amusement as he wiped the floor with her ass. People were trying to pull him off her, but he was on her ass like white on rice. When I thought she had enough and I heard someone call the police, I packed up my food and grabbed his ice cream. I jogged over and broke through the crowd that had formed around them.

"Lola, come on before your wild ass goes to jail and I have to bail you out!" I barked. I knew hearing the word jail would get his attention. He gave Tiffani one more good, hard slap and got off her. He scurried over to me and took his ice cream. "Hold this too."

I knew Roman would kill me for this, but I had to do it. This hoe had tried me too many times, so I guess the first beating wasn't enough. I waited until they helped her to her feet before calmly walking over and punching her square in the face. Her eyes crossed and she fell to the ground.

"That's for burning my shop down, hoe. Come *anywhere* near me or mine again and watch what the fuck I do," I threatened with venom spewing from my tone. I fixed my appearance, tossed my hair over my shoulder, and switched away. She could kiss my ass too!

SINCERE

I was sitting outside Kacey's house in my car, smoking before I went inside. I knew she was pissed at me for standing her up that night, but I had no choice. Jersey and Jo's lives were in danger for the second time. Choosing them was a no brainer for me. Plus, I wasn't quite ready to face Kacey after she up and kissed me suddenly. I can't front like I didn't enjoy it, and so did my third leg. It was a natural reaction to someone I was attracted to, and I was damn sure attracted to her. I just wasn't trying to see her like that. I wanted to continue building a friendship before taking that step — if we did.

Putting the roach in my ashtray, I popped some mint gum into my mouth to mask the funk of loud and sprayed on some cologne. I got out the car and locked my doors. I stood outside for a minute to air out some of the smell lingering on me, but it was too cold for this shit. I jogged up her steps and rang the doorbell, bouncing slightly to keep warm. Seconds later, she opened the door with an unpleasant expression. The heat leaving out the door was beckoning me to go inside. I looked at her with wide eyes and she moved to the side to let me in.

"I'm surprised you remember your way here, Sincere. You know, I haven't talked to you in days and you never showed up," she started before the door could shut good. It made me want to walk right back out the door and say fuck it, but I valued our friendship and knew we needed to talk about this.

"I know what I did, Kacey, and I apologize. Some shit came up that I had to handle," I explained.

"Like what?"

"Something with Jersey and Josiah."

"I knew it; like always," she mumbled under her breath while shaking her head. "It's always got something to do with her."

"Aye, if you're about to be trippin' like this, then I can bounce. I didn't come over here to argue with you; I just wanted to explain and apologize. You're actin' like we're a couple or something."

"So, tell me how you really feel," she spat and started to walk away. I reached out and gently grabbed her arm to stop her.

"My bad, baby girl. I didn't mean for it to come out like that," I sighed.

"But it did, Sin. It came out exactly how you meant it."

"And how do you think I meant it?"

"It's obvious you don't want to be with me. You're still in love with her, and that's fine. Just know I can't be your friend with the feelings I have for you. It would be fake of me to be on the sidelines secretly wishing I was her; wishing I had you," she whispered the last part and for some reason, it made my dick jump. How she said it with so much heart, so much feeling had me rethinking our relationship.

"What makes you think I'm still in love with her?"

"Because! You run to her every beck and call!"

"She is the mother of my child, what else am I supposed to do? Leave her out there to fend for herself? Fuck that! This shit is beyond her. It all boils down to that little boy that we share. Every breath I take, every move I make is for him. If you can't understand that, then there's no need for us to even be friends," I gave it to her straight.

Yeah, I still loved Jersey and would do what I could for her, but no one else mattered more than Josiah. He was my heart, and anyone that wanted to be in my life had to love him more than me, real shit. If he didn't approve of you, then it was an automatic no for me. He opinion meant more to me than anything and he was only four, but kids could read people and had no filter.

Kacey shocked me by crying. It tugged at my heartstrings seeing her tore up like she was, so I pulled her into my chest and wrapped my arms around her.

"Why you cryin', Kacey?"

"Be... because, I'm sorry. I... I didn't think of it like that. I... I was just... jealous," she admitted as she tried to catch her breath. "I'm so mad at myself for catching feelings for you when I promised myself not to, but I can't help it. I had a crush on you when we were younger, and all those feelings and butterflies came back when I saw you at the bar that day. My motive was to get closer to you and see where things would go."

"Why couldn't you tell me all this shit from the start?"

"You were so adamant about us just being friends that I went with it, just to be close to you," she answered as she laid her head on my chest. "I hope I didn't ruin our friendship." We stood there embracing one another in silence. I was in deep thought and she was waiting for me to say something.

"You didn't ruin anything. I'm always going to be your friend, Kacey. I just... I just can't take it to that level with you. I'm sorry because I know it hurts to hear that, but I'd rather keep it real with you than lie. What kind of friend would I be?" I pondered, and she laughed a little. "There she goes."

"You always know what to say, Sin; even when I don't want to hear it." I wasn't prepared for what happened next. She gazed up at me with those round brown eyes, and they were filled with lust. We stared at one another for a few seconds before she eased on her tiptoes and kissed me. The taste of strawberries on her succulent lips drove me crazy and things got intense.

I grabbed the back of her head and our kiss deepened. In the blink of an eye, our clothes were scattered all over the floor and I had her leaned over the couch, pounding her from behind. She was throwing it back and that shit felt good as fuck. The arch in her back was perfect and I was tapping her spot with each stroke. It was like this for hours; round after round, all over her house. Eventually, we made it to her room, where she tapped out and we both went to sleep.

I woke up the next morning filled with regret when I remembered what went down last night. Fuck! That was not supposed to happen. I knew I had just made things more complicated for her, and I didn't want that. I was clear about us just being friends, but she had to think otherwise now. Friends didn't do what we did and enjoy it. I know I sure did. Kacey's pussy was A1, and that was dangerous. That was my first and last time getting up in her.

"Good morning," Kacey greeted from the doorway. She was up and fully dressed, so I figured she was about to go to work. I got up and stretched so I could go home and shower.

"Good morning, baby girl. You about to head to work?" I asked as I found my clothes and shoes. I could feel her eyes on my body as I put on my clothes. I brushed her off and continued as if she wasn't there.

"Yes, but I was hoping we could talk first."

Aw, hell. I hope she wasn't about to ask what last night meant because to me, it didn't mean anything and I hate that I did it to begin with. I fell for the temptation.

"What's up?"

"I know what happened last night doesn't change the way you feel and as a grown woman, I can accept that and admit I was in need. It's been a while and I couldn't resist you."

"It's the same here, but we can never allow that to happen again. Sex is something that will damn sure ruin our friendship and I don't want that," I expressed, and she nodded her head in agreement.

"It won't. I can control myself now that I've had some," she giggled and I laughed.

I was relieved that she wasn't in here trying to read more into it than what it was. We were both grown enough to put this behind us and keep it moving. I found my phone and keys and we walked out together. I opened her car door for her and she gave me a hug. I kissed her forehead and gave her a weak smile.

"Have a good day at work. Hit me up when you get off."

"Thanks, and I will," she promised. She got in her car and I shut the door, then got into mine. I stopped to grab some breakfast for Jersey, Jo, and I before going home. I couldn't help but wonder how Jersey felt about me not coming back last night. For some reason, I felt rueful; like I had cheated on her. I had no reason to feel like that. We weren't together.

I pulled up to the house to see that her car was gone. I figured she had gone out to get something to eat, so I called her to let her know I had us some food. The phone rang once and went straight to voicemail. I tried again and someone answered the phone, but didn't say anything.

"Hello?" I said.

"Sin! What you doing?" Josiah asked while laughing.

"Nothing, little man. Why are you answering your mommy's phone?"

"Because, she told me to."

"Where are y'all?"

"At our house. All my toys are here!" he cooed, but I was stuck on his first statement.

"At your house? You're not at my house anymore, buddy?" I asked.

"Not uh. We weft (left) earwier (earlier)," he explained.

"Put mommy on the phone, please."

"Okay," he said and I heard his hard footsteps through the phone as I assumed he was running through the house. "Here you go, Mommy. Sin want talk to you."

"Hello, Sincere," Jersey greeted dryly.

"What are you doing? Why aren't y'all here?" I rambled, growing frustrated. I was so used to Josiah being at my house that I was in my feelings about him being gone. I wasn't feeling this.

"We came home. Everything is over and done with now, so it was time for us to leave."

"You know y'all didn't have to go, right? I didn't mind y'all being here."

"I know and I appreciate everything you've done for us, Sincere. I truly do and I promise I will repay you for it all. It was just time for us to come home. You and I both need our own privacy," she expressed.

"You're not repaying me for anything, Jay. It's my job to protect my son. Don't ever say you'll pay me back for doing my job," I explained while massaging my temples. I was getting frustrated at how she was talking. I felt like she was doing it on purpose to get under my skin. She knew how I was when it came to people I cared about. I would go above and beyond to make sure they were always straight. There was no price to pay, but to do the same in return.

"Whatever," she grumbled.

"Well, since you took Jo from me, can you at least start letting him stay the night? I'm used to spending time with him more now, and I don't want that to stop."

The most hurtful thing about them moving out was her taking Jo. I know that's where he belonged, but he had a father now who wanted to be an active part in his life. I adored my little man and didn't plan on going a day without seeing him. If she still wasn't comfortable with him staying the night, which I wouldn't see why she would be, then I would go pick him up every day. It was time for me to go meet with my lawyer and see how the adoption process was and what I needed to do.

"Let me think about it, okay? It's not you, I just don't want him out of my sight yet."

"And you think I do?"

"Don't do that, Sincere."

"What? I was just saying, Jay. I love him just like you do. He's my son too, whether you want to accept it or not. Let me be the father he needs. You know no one can protect him like us." The line grew quiet and I thought she had hung up until I heard Jo screaming at his toys in the background. I waited patiently for her to respond. She knew I was right.

"Okay. How about this... I go back to the doctor next week to see if I will be released to go back to work. If so, I will let him come spend the night with you," she finally spoke, and I was giddy as fuck.

I was about to go in and plan us a nice boy's night; just Jo and I.

Man, it was going to be the best night of my life and hopefully, it would be one of the best nights of his too. We were going to have so much fun that he wasn't going to want to go home. He could come live with me forever if he wanted, but I knew his mama wasn't having that, so I would settle for this. That is, until I adopted him and then, Jersey and I would have to come to an agreement on how we would share him. I wasn't going to be greedy, but I wanted all the time with my little man I could get.

"Aight, that sounds cool with me. Thank you," I thanked her with a smile.

"You're welcome. I'll talk to you later, okay?"

"Bet. Tell Jo I love him and I'll come see him later, if that's okay with you."

"That's fine with me, Sincere."

"Bet."

We ended the call and I was content with the outcome. Grabbing all the food, I got out and went inside my empty house. Damn, this was going to take some getting used to.

6

JERSEY

Two weeks later...

I was free and happy. The doctor gave me the okay to go back to work, and I couldn't be more excited. Work would be the perfect distraction to keep my mind clear and not think about these horrible things that had occurred over the last few months. I was just thankful to be able to say that the storm was over now and things were starting to feel normal again. Jo and I were getting back into our regular routine, and it felt good.

"Mommy, I ready to go" Jo announced as he made his way into my bathroom. I was putting the finishing touches on my makeup and peered at him through my mirror and laughed so hard. My baby had dressed himself and was looking rough. It was cute, though. I grabbed my phone and snapped a picture, then sent it to Sincere and Amari. No sooner than I sent it, my phone rang and it was Amari.

"Helloooo?" I answer cheerfully.

"Someone is chipper this morning. What are you doing up so early?"

"I go back to work today, remember?" I reminded her.

"Oh, snap! I forgot. And you're excited about that?"

"You know how it is when you're doing something you love."

"You got that right," she sighed. "I can't wait to tattoo again. It's been way too long and I'm scared I've lost my touch."

"Girl, please. Once you have it, you always will. You're amazing at what you do, Mari. No gift like that can be forgotten," I reassured her as I went to Jo's room to find him some more clothes.

"Thanks, cousin. I'm just nervous about how this grand opening is going to go. Lola and I have been working our asses off to get things done, and I can finally see things coming together."

"Don't be stressing my baby out, now. I need her to be stress free," I giggled. I wanted Amari to have a girl so bad. She would be beautiful just like her mama.

"Can I be honest with you?"

Uh oh. This doesn't sound good.

"Always."

"I've been trying not to stress over this whole sickle cell thing, but it's hard. I'm so afraid, Jersey, and I know it's not good for the baby. I just can't help it," she confessed with a sigh.

As a mother, I could understand where she was coming from. No good parent wanted their child to go through such a thing like that. We wanted our children to be healthy and happy, but unfortunately, it wasn't always like that for everyone. Some were forced to deal with seeing their child go through such horrible diseases and cancers. Working in the hospital, I saw it almost every day and it was so heartbreaking. That's why I always thanked God that Josiah was healthy. Amari had to pray over her baby that he or she would come out just fine.

"Stop that, Mari. That's not good for you or the baby. You're going to drive yourself crazy thinking about it. You just need to pray over the baby every day and ask God not to put too much on you that you can't handle, okay?" I advised as I put Jo's clothes on and headed out the door. I had another hour until I had to be at work, but I knew the early morning traffic would be hell and I wanted to make it on time.

"Okay, I will. I'm going to let you concentrate on the road. Kiss Jo for me and have a good first day back."

"I'll try. I love you."

"I love you too, hoe."

I threw my phone in the front seat as I buckled Jo in when I heard a car pull up behind me. I looked out the back window to see Sincere get out his car, and I licked my lips. He was so damn fine and I wanted him so bad, but I told myself not to beg anymore, especially since he was with a new woman. That was still hard for me to swallow, but it is what it is.

"Hey, I was just about to bring him to you," I stated as he walked over to my car. Jo's little sleepy eyes gleamed in excitement and he unbuckled his seatbelt.

"Hey, Sin! I go with you today," he exclaimed with a smile. "Bye, Mommy."

"Oh, so it's like that?" I chuckled and faked cried. Jo leaned over and hugged me, patting my back. I loved when he did that.

"I sorry, Mommy. You said I going with him today."

"You are, baby. Mommy was just playing," I giggled.

"Siwwy (silly) Mommy," Jo cracked up laughing, then reached for Sincere.

"You know he's too big to be picking up now, right?" I shook my head at how spoiled Sincere had him.

"He's cool. He's not heavy," Sincere dismissed with a smirk. "You must not have gotten my text."

"Oh, shit. I forgot to read it. Amari called and I never looked at it," I admitted and scrolled through my phone to see where he texted and said he would pick him up so I could get through all the traffic. It was sweet of him to be considerate like that, which he always was. That's one thing I had grown to love about him. "Thank you, Sincere. I appreciate you doing this."

"No biggie. Anything for my little man. You hungry?" he asked Jo, who nodded his head eagerly. As if on cue, my stomach growled, which caused Jo to bust out laughing.

"That was Mommy's bewwy (belly)."

"I guess he's not the only one," Sincere chuckled. "Come on, we can go grab y'all something to eat before you go in. You have enough time, right?"

As bad as I wanted to take him up on his offer, I declined. I was going to let them have their alone time and I could eat at work. Also, I didn't want to start back spending time with Sincere. Living with him was a job of its own, and I was just now starting to get over the feeling of missing him. I walked them to the car and kissed Jo, then thanked Sincere for keeping him while I was working.

"I'll be there to get him as soon as I get off," I yelled over my shoulder.

"No, you won't. He's spending the night with me, remember?"

Shit! I forgot I had agreed to that. I was already looking forward to getting off and spending time with Josiah, but I was going to keep my word and let him stay. I knew that Jo would love that, and I could use some me time.

"Oh, yeah. I forgot; sorry. I'll... uhm... come pick him up tomorrow when I get off."

"I'll bring him to you when he's ready to come home," he said and I wanted to protest, but kept my mouth shut and agreed. I didn't feel like arguing or anything. I was in a good mood and knew Jo was in great hands. He wanted to stay just as bad as Sincere wanted him to.

We went our separate ways and thankfully, traffic wasn't too bad and I made it to work at a reasonable time. I hopped out my car and went inside, anxious to see everyone. I was greeted with love, hugs, and sympathy cards. No one knew what I really went through but Mama Edith, and she didn't know everything. Not even Eli knew, and that's how I wanted it to stay. They all thought that I got in a bad car accident when I went on vacation. If they only knew.

I walked into my joint office with Eli to find his things gone. His desk, filing cabinet, computer; all those things are more. It was set up different, with my desk sitting in the far-left corner. What was going on here? I set my things down and headed down to the cafeteria to see Mama Edith. I missed her and I knew she would be the one to tell me what was going on.

I inhaled deeply as I walked through the doors. The fresh smell of coffee and cinnamon greeted me. I never realized how much I missed work until now. Coming down to the cafeteria had always been one of my favorite parts of my work day, and it felt good to be back.

"You're back!" Mama Edith exclaimed when she saw me. She took off her gloves and apron and came trotting over to me. We embraced one another tightly, and it felt good to be in her arms again.

"Yes ma'am," I breathed with a smile as we pulled away from one another. "You know I had to come pop up on my favorite woman."

"I'm glad you did, baby. You just made my entire day. How are you feeling?"

"A lot better," I answered honestly, and I meant that physically and mentally. My chest would be sore sometimes, but other than that, I was fine. "I'm happy to be back at work. I was getting bored not doing anything."

"I'm sure you had plenty to do with Josiah," she chuckled. "Speaking of my little handsome baby, I miss him. Where is he?"

"He missed you too, and he's with Sincere today."

"And how are things going between the two of you?" I was hoping she wouldn't ask me that, but I knew better.

"We're not together anymore." I kept my answer short and simple. I wasn't in the mood to talk about it, and I hoped she didn't press the issue. I guess she caught the hint because she just left it at that and boy, was I thankful.

"What is meant to be, will be. Don't forget that," she stated with hope filled eyes. "Now, let me get back to work, baby. I don't trust anyone making the cinnamon rolls but me," she giggled and so did I. She didn't play about her cooking.

"Yes ma'am. Oh, I meant to ask you, where's Eli? It was only my desk in there," I said.

"They were finally able to clear out a space so y'all wouldn't have to share anymore. Eli remembered how you would always say you wanted to stay in the office if they ever found another one, so he moved his things," she explained. I owed Eli for this one. When he wasn't being perverted, he was a good person and sweet man. He would make a woman happy one day if he ever got his shit together, but I doubt he would.

"I owe him for that. Is he here today?"

"No. He's off today, but he'll be here tomorrow."

We chatted a little more before she heard a timer going off and scurried away. I went to my office and done some rearranging to my liking and started going over my paperwork before going to see my first patient. It was a busy day, but that's how I loved for things to be. It always made the day go by and before I knew it, it was time to clock out and go home. Since it was just me tonight, I stopped by the liquor store to get a bottle of wine. My feet were aching and I just wanted to soak in a nice, hot bubble bath and drink half the bottle of wine. It would help me sleep good.

I was on my second glass of wine and my water was starting to get cold. Just as I was about to let the water out and start the shower, my phone started ringing. My mother's ringtone blared and I was confused. It was late and she never called after a certain time. I quickly dried off my hands and answered.

"Hey, Mama."

"Hey, Jersey. How are you feeling, baby?" She sniffled and her voice croaked, so I knew something was wrong.

"Mama, are you okay? Are you crying?"

"No," she admitted and started crying harder. "I need you so bad right now."

Hearing her say that broke my heart. Whatever buzz I had was now gone and replaced with worry. I couldn't stand hearing my mama break down like this and not be anywhere near to soothe her.

"Mama, stop crying. I'm sorry; just tell me what's wrong."

"It... it's Don, baby. He... uh.... today, we found out he has stage three lung cancer."

"Are you serious?" I whispered in disbelief. Don was such a healthy man. He takes great care of himself and his body, but that didn't matter to cancer.

"Yes," she sniffled. "I'm so tore up, Jersey. I don't know what to do."

"I'm so sorry, Mama. I wish I was there with you. It's killing me that I'm not there to be your shoulder to lean on," I stated in a sympathetic tone. I know I just started back at work, but I needed to go be there for my mama and Don. I knew how she was, and she needed me there to be strong for her.

"Can you please come back, baby? Just for a few months to see how his progress goes. I can't do this alone."

A few months? I didn't expect that. Maybe a week, but a few months was too long. My career was here in Birmingham, and I had started a life here. I didn't want to go back to New Jersey and start all over again. Amari and I had grown closer and Josiah had formed a bond with Sincere. I wasn't taking my baby away from the only father figure he's ever had, but I can't just leave my mama hanging when she needs me the most. God, what was I going to do?

KENDRICK

I woke up and found myself still at the hospital. I sighed heavily and closed my eyes again. The dream I had felt all too real. In it, I was released from the hospital and went home, where I was so desperately ready to be. I was ready to sleep in my own bed and feel comfortable. I missed being in my own space. I got tired of nurses coming in and out all times of the day and night. It was annoying.

To my surprise, my room was free of any visitors. Usually when I woke up, my parents or Amari would be sitting and waiting for me to wake it. I can't lie and say waking up to an empty room wasn't welcoming. Don't get me wrong, I appreciated them more than they knew, but sometimes I just wanted to be alone, like now. It gave me time to clear my mind and cope with my situation.

Every day I woke up, I prayed that my feeling came back in my upper body. It had been challenging not being able to do for myself. Someone had to feed and bathe me. I couldn't feel when anyone hugged me and that shit hurt, especially when it was Keyana and Hayden. Keyana was old enough to understand, but not Hayden. One day, he got so upset I didn't hug him back that he started throwing a fit. Dad explained to him the best he could about my situation. After they all left that night, I laid here and cried. Why did this have to happen to me? Why was I suffering?

"Good morning, Kendrick." The morning nurse greeted with a smile and food. "I'm surprised no one is here."

"Good morning and trust me, someone will be here soon." I chuckled and laid back as she checked my vitals. This was routine and I still wasn't used to it. I'd much rather be at home.

"Are you getting any feeling back in your upper body?" she quizzed as she jotted a few notes down on her chart.

"No," I sighed in disappointment. "What's taking so long? I hate lying here like a vegetable with a brain."

She snickered a little and I had to laugh myself. As I thought about it, I knew I needed to stop complaining and just be thankful that I was alive. Some people in my situation didn't always survive, so even though I was paralyzed, I was still alive and that was all that mattered. I had to stop and thank God for life.

"There's no time frame on when it will come back. It all just depends on your body and what it wants to do," she explained with a weak smile. "Don't worry. Just give it time. It will come."

"I hope so."

"Would you like to eat?"

"No, thank you."

"Are you sure?"

"Yeah." I wasn't trying to be rude or anything. I just wanted to be alone for a little longer until someone came.

"Okay. You know what to do if you need me. I'll be back a little later to give you your meds and check on you," she said before leaving out the room.

Thank God.

Knock knock!

Damnit. "Come in."

The door opened and in walked Harmony. She was looking much better and even more beautiful to me. Her face was healing well, except for some faded bruises and scars. She had her hair pulled into a bun on the top of her head and she had on a little makeup. She wore a Houndstooth sweater with all black leggings and white Nikes. I couldn't stop staring at her. For some reason, I was feeling a little different about her today; like, I was actually happy to see her. It reminded me of when we were in a good place in our relationship. I remember when I couldn't wait to get off work and see her. I would hurry home just to be around her. I missed that with her.

Before she changed, Harmony was always down for me. She was always down for whatever I was. At that time, she was real deal wifey material. She cooked, cleaned, and took care of me while I worked. Now, I didn't always just let her do it. Just because I was working didn't mean I couldn't help around the house. Her and I both lived there, so we both had to take care of it. When it all boiled down to it, other than our kids, those memories and years invested are what allowed me to finally forgive her.

"Hey, Ken."

"What's up, Harm. You're up here early today," I noted with a smile.

"You asked me to come early so I could come bathe you instead of the nurse, remember?" she reminded me.

I had completely forgot, but I was glad she remembered. I hated when the nurses bathed me. It was already bad enough that I couldn't do it myself, but it was much worse with a stranger doing it. Mama and Dad would do it while they were here too, but it was just weird to me because I'm a grown ass man. I didn't want my mama seeing my private areas. Yeah, I know she saw them before me, but that was a long ass time ago and I wasn't small anymore, if you catch my drift.

"Oh, yeah. My bad. I appreciate you coming through for me."

"You know I got you, Ken. So, is everything in the bathroom?" she asked as she got out some clean clothes for me.

"Yeah."

My eyes followed the switch of her hips as she trotted to the bathroom. Damn. I may be paralyzed permanently from the waist down, but that didn't stop my mans from springing into action. I glanced down and saw my bulge poking through the blanket. He was in need of some desperate attention. It had been too damn long since I got my dick wet, and Harmony was the last person I fucked. I had to close my eyes and think about something other than her riding me.

"You ready?" she startled me and I opened my eyes to see she wasn't looking at my face, but at what was poking against the cover. She was damn near drooling, so I cleared my throat to get her attention.

"I'm ready."

She nodded her head and started taking my clothes off. I had to keep my eyes shut as she bathed me. I didn't want us making eye contact and I brick up again. I was semi soft now, but I knew that would change when I looked at her. The attraction I had for her was at an all-time high, and I wasn't trying to reveal that just yet. We still had a long way to go before I considered going there with her. It didn't hurt to think about it, though.

Just as she was finishing up, there was a knock at the door and then it opened. Amari waltzed in with a smile, until she saw Harmony putting my clothes on. She kissed her teeth loudly and sat in the seat next to the window without saying anything. I was over her and her little funky ass attitude whenever Harmony was in the room. I knew if she wasn't helping me right now, then she would have left as soon as she saw Amari. That's just how it was, and that's why she avoided being around her. Let me just say, I don't blame her. I knew how Mari was and her little self was very intimidating. Plus, Harm knew firsthand how Mari threw hands; just saying.

"It's rude to come see someone and not speak, Amari," I said, and she rolled her eyes.

"Hey, Ken," she spoke dryly.

"Am I the only person you see in the room?" I quizzed with a raised brow.

"The only person I care to see."

"You have to stop with this shit, sis. This is getting out of hand."

"It's been out of hand! You should have been telling her that!" she yelled and scooted to the edge of her seat.

"Don't you think I know that already?" Harmony chimed in, snapping her neck to look at Mari and shocking the hell out of me. She was taking up for herself for the first time in a while. Usually, Harm was all mouth and would pop back off at Mari quick. Since she had been feeling guilty and scared, she had been walking on eggshells when she came. Not anymore, and I was ready to see how this was going to play out.

"Apparently not. You wouldn't have done all the fucked-up shit you did," Mari spat back calmly, folding her arms across her bosom.

"Oh my gosh! Amari, I am sorry! I don't know how many times you want to be say it, but I will say it again; I'm sorry! Like I told your brother, I've done some fucked up shit, I know that. I also know that I can't take any of it back as bad as I want to. I just want you and your parents to forgive me and give me another chance, like Kendrick has. I don't understand why it's so hard for y'all, but not him."

"Oh, you don't?" Mari challenged with a raised brow.

"No, I don't. I think it should have been the hardest for him and easier for y'all, but apparently, I was wrong."

"I have every gotdamn reason to hold a grudge if I want to! You must have thought I didn't know about you playin' a part in my shop burnin' down."

"Whoa, what?" I asked. This was news to me, and not good at all. No wonder Amari wasn't trying to hear shit about forgiving Harm.

"Yup. I bet when you were confessing your shit, you left out that little piece of information, huh?" Mari taunted Harmony with a pleased smirk tugging at her lips. Harm was on mute as she looked back and forth between the two of us, so Mari continued. "You must have not told him how you were the mastermind behind it all. How *you* went to that bitch Tiffani and told her *you* wanted to hit me where it hurt, so *you* burned my shop down. Well, jokes on you, bitch. That did nothing but bless me with something better and put more coins in my bank account. So, I guess I should thank you for failing."

"Did you do that, Harm?" I questioned her as she stood there crying silently. She peered at me and nodded her head yes.

"Damn... now, I see why you feel like you do. My bad, sis," I apologized to Mari.

"It's cool. You didn't know and I never said anything." She

brushed it off, but I knew she was feeling some type of way. I had been hard on her about forgiving Harmony and never stopped to think that maybe it was deeper than the shit she had done to me. "I'll be back later, Ken. Tell a nurse to call me when she leaves."

With that being said, Amari got up and stormed out the room. I knew she wouldn't be back until tomorrow, and I was going to allow her some time to cool off so we could talk about it without getting heated; well, her anyway. I just wanted to apologize again, but she would have a lecture for me whenever she came back.

"That was some foul shit, Harm. Fuckin' up my sister's business because you were jealous? That's foul, man," I fussed while shaking my head.

"I know," she whimpered. "I swear I will get a job and pay for everything."

"It's already taken care of, but don't expect her to come around anytime soon. Amari holds grudges for a long ass time and you destroyed something very important to her. I don't know if you can make up for that," I kept it real with her. She needed to know what would happen.

"I pray I can."

"Me too. I'll talk to her."

"Thank you, Ken. I don't know what I would do without you," she expressed and walked over to kiss my forehead.

Shit with her wasn't perfect, but I was happy with where we were and wanted things to get better. My next step was to get my parents to sit down and talk with her. Everyone needed to be cordial for the sake of Keyana and Hayden, and I don't think that would be possible until everyone got everything off their chests. Amari did, so it was Mama and Dad's turn. I would talk to them about it later.

Out of nowhere, I started feeling funny. I could feel. My upper body was tingling severely, like when your foot falls asleep. I wanted to get excited, but not too excited. Could this be? Was I really getting my feeling back?

"Harm, call the nurse," I demanded.

"What's wrong? Are you okay?" she panicked as she repeatedly hit the call button. No one answered, but my nurse from earlier jogged into the room.

"Is everything okay?" she asked with wide eyes.

"Uhm, I'm not sure. He just asked me to call you," Harmony explained as she gazed at me with concern.

"What's going on, Kendrick?" the nurse questioned.

"My upper body is tingling," I said, and a smile crossed her lips.

"That's a good thing. Let me go get Dr. Kennings so she can check you out." She left and came back with Dr. Kennings moments later.

"I hear we may have some good progress, Kendrick," Dr. Kennings beamed as she washed her hands. "So, you're feeling some tingling, correct?"

"Yes."

"Feeling is a great sign. Are you in pain?"

"No, just tingling."

"And that's even better. Tell me, can you feel this?" she interrogated as she ran her pen up and down my hair. The feeling was light, but it was there, which caused me to grin.

"Just a little, but I can feel it," I answered eagerly.

"Welp, there it is," Dr. Kennings chuckled. "You are officially getting you feeling back. I'm not going to overwork you today since it's just coming back, but tomorrow we can do some exercises to get those limbs and muscles loose."

That was the best thing I'd heard since I woke up. Soon, I would be able to hug my kids and feel it. I would be able to wrap my arms around them. Man, God is always on time. I couldn't help but cry. I was overwhelmed with so much happiness.

"Oh, don't cry," Harmony said, but she was crying too.

"I can't help it. It's been a long time coming."

"It has, but you're making excellent progress. With you regaining feeling, you can start rehab and that means you're closer to going home. First, I want to see how you do with pain. You've healed a great deal, but I just like to be safe," Dr. Kennings explained with a smile. "Congrats, Kendrick. You're doing awesome."

"Thank you, Dr. Kennings. For everything."

"Hey, it's my job. Plus, I love being able to take care of and help people. I love what I do, and I love getting to know my patients. Overtime, they become family," she answered, and I could see that she was genuine.

Things could go nowhere but up from here.

MARISSA

My face was finally healed from Amari's sucker punch. For her to be so small, she sure packed a hard punch, which I can say I deserved. I'm just glad I no longer had to worry about that.

Frankie and I were better than ever since our little secret was out. I truly felt I made the right decision by choosing him and so far, he had been the best. We spent a lot of time together when we weren't working, and I had even met his family. I could see that things were getting serious fast, and it wasn't what I was used to in a relationship, but I welcomed the change with open arms.

The bell on the door to *Rissa's Sweets* went off, and in walked Olivia. I knew she was upset with me because she hadn't heard from me. Between making time for Frankie and work, I hardly had time to have a moment to myself. It was no excuse because she was a busy woman too and made time for me. She was here to get in my ass, so I put down the papers in my hand and walked to the back, away from the customers. Olivia could get loud and I didn't need her acting her color in front of everyone.

"You already know what's up," she started as she shut the door. "What's been up with you, Rissa? You haven't been returning my calls or texts, but I see you posting pictures with the doctor. Like, damn.

His dick that good you forgot about your *best* friend? The one who's been here long before him."

"I'm sorry, Olivia. I've been super busy and it feels like I haven't had time to do much but work."

"Bullshit, bitch. Apparently, you haven't been too busy if you find enough time to squeeze Frankie in. Come up with a better excuse."

"It's not an excuse."

"Then what is it? Because it damn sure ain't the truth. You know what, Rissa? You've changed. Since you started seeing Frankie, you haven't been the same. You dress different, you always wear makeup, and you've forgotten about the other people in your life. You're not the same Marissa Holden I've known since diapers. I know we grow up and things change, but I never expected it to be you," she accused with a deep scowl etched on her face.

"I'm sorry, bestie. I know I've been spending a lot of time with Frankie, but we're in a relationship; of course, we want to spend a lot of time together. Between me running my business and him being a doctor, any little time outside of those two things we get, we want to spend it with one another. No, I haven't forgot about you and I never will. It's just that I'm happy," I explained the best I could. At least I was being honest. Olivia knew I loved her, and that was what mattered, right? She stood there with her hands on her hips, shaking her head at me. "What?"

"You don't get it. I'm happy that you're happy, but you can be happy and still remember me. You don't always have to be under his ass, Marissa. You have a life outside of him too, in case you forgot."

"Whatever. You're just jealous. You're not really happy for me," I spat in anger. "Since Frankie and I first started talking, you've had nothing but negative things to say."

"Jealous? Tell me, what in the fuck do I have to be jealous about? Huh? Oh, because you're happy with a rich doctor and I'm not? Girl, please! I would hate to be in your shoes because you, my friend, are a low down dirty bitch for how you did Kendrick. You really think things between you and Frankie are going to work? Ha! You have to be one delusional bitch to believe that. Remember, there's a thing called karma, Marissa. You think since everything is out in the open that it will be all fine and dandy, but that's far from the truth, and don't come crying to me when shit starts falling about in your "relationship." I wish your business nothing but success, and I will always love you. I just can't deal with this unknown woman standing in front of me anymore."

Olivia stormed out my office in tears, leaving me there to soak in mine. I couldn't believe that just happened, but I knew it was coming eventually. Olivia was a ticking time bomb and always lashed out when things didn't go her way. I was truly hurt by her words and just wanted her to be happy for me. Did I really think she was jealous? No. I knew that was far from the truth, but that was the only thing I could think of at the moment to explain her behavior. Shit went way left and I would apologize soon. She needed time to cool off, and so do I.

I glanced down at my watch and saw it was Frankie's lunch time. Since I was in such a bad mood now, I decided to go sit with him to make me feel better. I went to the front to get his favorite cupcake to surprise him with. I told my manager I would be back in a few and headed to the hospital.

Like always, it was a crowded busy day and my mind drifted to Kendrick. Frankie had told me had been awake for a few weeks now, and I couldn't help but wonder how he was doing. In the back of my mind, I knew I owed him an apology and an explanation, but I was too scared and guilty to face him. I was positive Amari told him everything by now and he probably hated my guts, so I pushed that idea out my mind and went to find my man.

As I made my way to his office, some nurses smiled and waved, while others snarled their noses in disgust. I just shrugged them off and strutted to my man. I knew some of them were bitter about me locking Frankie down, but that wasn't my problem. He chose who he wanted, and they just had to deal with it.

When I made it to his office door, I was about to knock when an unfamiliar voice caught my attention. They giggled and I leaned my ear against the door to hear that they were inside with him. It was most definitely a female, so I barged in without knocking to see Frankie sitting cozy with the mystery woman, who was sitting in his lap. My heart shattered as I watched him cup the side of her face and they engaged in a kiss. They were so into one another that they didn't notice me standing there until I sent the cupcake flying at his head.

"Yo, what the- Marissa." He gulped with wide, guilty eyes. He pushed the woman off him and stood to his feet. "Listen, baby. I can explain."

"Explain? Explain what, Frankie? What I just saw is enough explanation," I stated as I held back tears and swallowed the lump in my throat. I was broken, but I wouldn't dare let him see.

"It's not what it looks like," he gave me that old tired line and I had to laugh. I couldn't believe he had me fooled. I was blind, but now, he was showing me his true colors and he was just like the rest.

"What do you mean it's not what it looks like?" The woman scoffed with hurt dripping from her tone. "We've been seeing each other for weeks now, Frankie. How are you just going to brush it off like it's nothing?"

"Wow," I breathed in disbelief as I grilled his guilty ass. He was on mute and couldn't say anything after that. There wasn't anything else for him to say. He was busted, and his secret was now out. He had been playing one hell of a good game, but I would no longer be a participant. I was done. "So, this is how you do me? After all the shit I risked being with you, you turn around and play me for a fool, Frankie? Really?"

"I'm sorry, Marissa. I... I didn't mean for shit to come out like this. I truly care about you and I want to make things work. The plan today was to break things off with her so I could fully be with you," he stammered a lie straight through his teeth.

"Oh, really? That's not what you were just telling me! We were in here discussing our future right before she came in," the woman cried as she stood up and slapped the fire out of him. "You know what, this is not what I came for. Delete my number and forget about me. Don't come down to my office looking for me or trying to make amends. I'm done with you for good this time, Frankie. Fool me once, shame on you. Fool me twice, shame on me. This is the third time, so I guess that makes me dumb for believing you changed after the first two times. You're nothing but a low down dirty nigga that needs to grow the fuck up and be a man. Stop acting like a little ass teenage boy," she spat, slapping him once more and then turning to me. "I'm sorry about all this. I had no clue about you, and it's obvious you didn't know about me. Frankie and I have been off and on for two years now, and I thought this time he had changed. Apparently not. My advice to you is to run and never look back at this scumbag. He's not worth the heartache and pain, believe me. You're beautiful, girl, and I'm positive you can find someone better."

She glanced at him once more before grabbing her purse and storming out, with me right behind her.

"Wait, Marissa. Please, don't leave. Let's sit down and talk it out." Frankie stopped me by grabbing my arm, but I snatched it away.

"Don't you fuckin' touch me. I'm disgusted with you and I never want to see you again. I risked so much to be with you, and look how you did me. I believed in you, in us. I thought I had found the one, but you're for everybody. Fuck you, Frankie."

I ran out the room before he could get another word in. I found the bathroom and thanked God it was empty. I locked myself in a stall and broke down. How did I miss this? Frankie was good at keeping his tracks covered and putting on a different persona. I was sick to my stomach, literally. I emptied the contents of my stomach into the toilet and thought about the decisions I had made. Olivia and I were on bad terms because of him and I hated to admit it, but she was right. I couldn't be mad at anyone but myself for how I went about everything. I turned my back on Ken when he needed me the most and pushed Olivia to the side, all for what? For my own selfish reasons that came back to bite me in the ass. It was my punishment from God and best believe, I had learned my lesson.

Since I was at the hospital still, I thought it would be good to go see Kendrick and apologize. I needed to know he forgave me, so I could move on with life. After that, I would go find Olivia and do the same. I had made this mess, so I had to clean it up. It wouldn't be an easy clean up, but I had to start somewhere.

I took the elevator down to Ken's floor and went to his room. I said a silent prayer before knocking on the door and going inside to be met with the surprise of my life. Harmony was there, sitting by his bedside. When she glanced up at me, her facial expression changed, but she remained silent. That was a big difference from the Harmony I met at the restaurant that day. My eyes moved to Kendrick, who was grilling me with a look of pure hurt and disgust, which made me uncomfortable and second guess being here, but it was something I had to do.

"Why are you here, Marissa? Aren't you supposed to be somewhere under the doctor's ass?" Kendrick quizzed with venom spewing from his tone, which was expected.

"Uhm... I came here to apologize to you and your family. I... I know what I did was wrong and I'm so, so sorry. I never meant for things to happen like they did; they just happened. I lost control and made a poor decision that I truly regret," I expressed before I lost the courage to. The way him and Harmony were staring daggers through my body made things extremely awkward.

"You can take yourself and your fake ass, bullshit apology and get the fuck out my room. You weren't who you portrayed to be, and I don't want any parts in whatever you have going on. You chose who you wanted, and I'm cool with that. Yeah, it hurt, but it is what it is. I wish you and him nothing but the best. Now, you can excuse yourself. I'm good," he responded in a cold, even tone and looked at Harmony, who got up and opened the door for me with a smirk tugging at her lips.

"You are dismissed," she taunted while looking me in the eyes. "And please, don't come back or I will show you the Harmony you saw at the restaurant that day and trust, you don't want that girl to come back."

I took that as a warning and got the hell up out of there, leaving feeling worse than I already was. I couldn't be mad at anyone at myself. Seeing the hurt in Ken's hypnotizing hazel green eyes would haunt me for a while. Knowing it was because of me made me feel lower than low. This day had been pure hell, and I didn't think it could get any worse. I decided to just go home and sleep this feeling away. Hopefully, I would feel better in the morning.

I stepped off the elevator and since I wasn't looking where I was going, I bumped right into someone.

"I'm sorr—" I started and looked up, only to be met with eyes matching Ken's. Amari was standing there with her arms folded across her bosom and a mischievous grin. She checked her surroundings before shoving me back into the elevator and pushing the last floor.

WHAP!

"Ooo, I was hoping I would catch you again and today must be my lucky day," she cooed as she slapped my ass. "And bitch, I dare you to hit me back while I'm pregnant. I'll make the biggest scene and call the police."

My face was stinging and I was sobbing. I was scared for what she was about to do next, and even more worried because I couldn't defend myself. I wouldn't dare hit her knowing she was pregnant, but sometimes you had to do what you had to do. If she kept on, then I was going to have to give her a little taste of her own medicine.

"Please, just let me go home, Amari. I'm done and I will never bother you or your family again, I promise. Just don't hit me anymore," I begged.

She leaned back against the railing and glared at me while shaking her head. "I'm not going to fuck you up how I want to because I can't get too riled up. Steer clear and be mindful of your surroundings, hoe. You never know where I might be and best believe, after I drop this baby and I catch you out in the streets, be ready for me to light that ass up."

I nodded my head and she pressed the button for Ken's floor. The elevator stopped and she flipped her hair over her shoulder and started to get off, but stopped to look at me once more. "I hope he breaks your heart and stomps all over that shit. You don't deserve to be happy."

She walked away and I was thankful that she had spared me, once again. This is what happens when you do wrong. Nothing good comes from it and I knew that from the start, but I really knew now. I learned a valuable lesson from all this and took it to heart. I couldn't change my past, but I had a future to make things better.

7

HARMONY

*I*t was taking everything in me not to run out behind that bitch and fuck her up. Kendrick had told me everything that transpired between the two of them and I was livid that she would do something like that. Yeah, I know I done a lot worse, but to see someone else hurt him like that fucked with me. Since I was trying to show him I had changed and I wasn't the old Harmony, I refrained from dragging her all across that hospital. Plus, I knew Amari had already got in her ass and that was enough for anyone.

I sat back down next to Ken and began massaging his hands. Dr. Kennings suggested it to help with the tingling sensation, so I was constantly doing so. He wiggled his fingers a bit and I smiled. He was doing better and it was exciting for everyone; well, at least that's what he told me. I had yet to talk to his parents, but I knew it was coming soon.

"You okay?" I asked as I tried to read his mind by looking into his eyes. I knew he was upset because they were dark and unreadable.

"Yeah, just didn't expect to see her," he admitted with a sigh.

"Me either, but you set her straight. She's in the past, so don't worry about her anymore. You don't need any added stress," I advised him.

"I'm not. I'm just glad I said what I had to say to her. I know I will forgive her eventually, but I just can't right now."

"Like, with me?" I whispered with my head down. Ken says he forgives me, but deep in my heart, I know he's still struggling with the decision and I don't blame him. I'd done some horrible things.

"Don't start that, Harm. You know I forgive you."

"I know you're saying that, but do you believe it? Honestly."

"Yes, I do. Because if I didn't, you wouldn't be standing here right now." He chuckled and it made me giggle. I guess he was truly over it; if that's what he said, then I had no choice but to believe him.

"Okay." I let it go with a smile tugging at my lips. I pulled out my phone and saw it was time for me to go. I had somewhere to be and I couldn't be late. "Well, I'm about to go. I'll be back tomorrow, okay?"

"Alright. Be safe and please, consider coming when my parents are here so y'all can talk. You know they have Keyana and Hayden all the time, so you'll get to see them too," Ken pleaded.

"I'll think about it. I can't make any promises," I replied and he accepted that answer. I kissed his cheek and told him to call if he needed me. I gathered my things and headed out the door, running into Amari. She just rolled her eyes and walked around me. I shrugged my shoulders and went on my way. I wanted to beat the twelve o'clock lunch traffic, and I was pushing for time.

I made it to my destination twenty minutes later. I checked my appearance in the mirror and got out. The warm, inviting scent of cherry blossom kissed my nose as I walked inside. The place gave me good vibes, so I could relax and not be so nervous.

"Hi, I'm here to see Dr. Polin," I informed the receptionist.

"Your name?"

"Harmony Knight."

"Did you fill out the paperwork and questionnaire online?" she quizzed, and I nodded my head yes. Anything to speed up the process. "Okay, you may go on back. Dr. Polin is waiting for you."

I thanked her, then opened the door to my right that led straight into her office. The aroma of cherry blossom got stronger and I sneezed.

"Bless you," Dr. Polin said and laughed. "That's usually the first thing people do when they come in here. I've been trying to work on that," she stated with humor and stood up to hug me. "It's nice to meet you, Harmony. Have a seat. How are you today?"

"I'm good. Thank you for seeing me," I thanked her as I took a seat across from her. She sat down and folded her legs while writing something down on a notebook in her lap.

"This is how it will go. I will ask you a few questions to get you warmed up and then, we'll get deeper into things. I will be writing things down and recording our session. Is that fine with you? I like for my patients to be comfortable, and the information is confidential. It will only be between you and me," she explained.

"No, I don't mind."

"Okay, great. Let's get started. What brings you to see me today?"

Yes, I was seeing a psychologist. This is one thing I felt I needed to do in order to grow and also, get to the root of what caused me to do all I'd done; to find out where all the anger, animosity and jealousy came from. I wasn't only doing this for myself. I was also doing this for my kids and Kendrick. I felt like I owed them this.

"I've done some horrible things to the people I love, and I'm not sure why. Well, I have a clue, but I'm not sure why I feel those emotions," I started.

"What emotions?"

"Anger. Jealousy. Hate. I had no reason to take those emotions out on the people I did, but I just couldn't help it. It was all I could do."

"Explain to me those emotions. Tell me what each emotion caused you to do to hurt those people."

What did I sign myself up for? This was becoming a bit too much and personal for me, but I had to think about why and who I was doing it for. I swallowed my pride and started sharing some of my story.

"With anger, I would always lash out on my fiancé for no reason. Well, ex fiancé. Any little thing he did would trigger something inside of me. He could work all day to provide for me and my two children, and I would be angry because I felt like he didn't spend any time with us. No matter what it was, I would go off and then, go find comfort in the arms of someone else. It wasn't always like this. I just started to change over time."

"And, when did you notice this change?" she quizzed as she wrote something down.

"One day, after we had sex and I didn't want to, but I did it for him because I loved him. It wasn't like he pressured me or anything. It was a choice I made on my own."

"How was that sexual encounter with him?"

"Awful, and I felt so bad because he was so into it and I wasn't. It was just something about that day that had me off my square."

"So, after that sexual encounter, you developed the anger?"

"Yes."

"Mmhmm. How was your childhood, Harmony? Were you close with your parents? Do you have any siblings? How was your upbringing?"

My childhood was a touchy subject for me. It wasn't bad, but it wasn't great either. I had some trying, hard times that I didn't want to relive, so I pushed them to the back of my mind and continued living.

"My childhood was okay; it wasn't ideal, but okay. I was close with my mother, and my father was never in my life. I never had any siblings and I wanted them so bad because I hated being alone. I remember there were times I would beg my mother to give me a brother or sister, and she would just laugh it off. When she died from ovarian cancer, I knew why should couldn't. It wasn't until she was on her deathbed that she told me I was her miracle child. She wasn't supposed to have me, but she did."

I missed my mother so much, and that's why I never talked about her. It was too painful. Only Kendrick and Fancy knew about her because when I was vulnerable, I would talk to them about her. If anyone else asked about her, I would either act like I didn't hear them or just ignore them all together. It was just my way of doing things.

"I'm so sorry for your loss. I lost my mother not too long ago, and I understand that pain. It's almost unbearable, but somehow, we get through it. The pain never goes away, though. We just learn to ignore it sometimes," she sympathized with me and handed me some tissues. I didn't realize I was crying, but I wasn't surprised. It happened anytime I talked about her.

"Thank you."

"You're welcome. Did your mother have a boyfriend or a husband?"

"She was a lesbian, but she had some male friends that would come over."

"And where were you when they came over?"

"I would either be in my room or outside playing with my friends. Mama never wanted me around them because I developed at an early age. She was always afraid of someone... someone taking advantage of me."

"Did anyone take advantage of you?"

"Yes," I cried while trying to shake off the pain that was resurfacing.

"How old were you?"

"Which time?"

"How many times has it happened?" she asked in concern.

"Three times. Once when I was twelve, sixteen, and a few weeks ago." I was sobbing by now as flashbacks of each time replayed in my head. The image of each man breathing heavily in my face haunted me every time I blinked.

"Where was your mother when you were twelve and sixteen? Did you ever tell anyone?"

"No."

"And why not?"

"Because, they always made it seem like it was my fault. Like I asked to be my size and built like I am. They would threaten me whenever they saw me and being a young girl, I believed them. Being picked on at school didn't make it any better. People would always tease me; especially other girls. After my second time being raped, I just started having sex with any guy that asked because I was scared they would take it. I thought I was doing the right thing, but it made things worse. I would continuously be in fights for trying to defend myself, my name, and to prove to the other girls I wasn't scared so they could leave me alone."

This was hard to talk about, but a relief all in one. The more I talked, the more the weight felt lighter. Dr. Polin was doing an excellent job at getting to the root of my problems, and I couldn't thank her enough. Before I knew it, our hour was up and it was time for me to go. It was so easy talking to her because I knew she wasn't judging me. She was the one person who didn't know me from a can of paint that let me just be so open, and because I was paying her to do so. Still, it meant a lot to me.

"Thank you so much for this. I feel better than when I first came in," I told her with a smile as we hugged.

"Will you be back next week?" she asked, hopeful.

"Same time," I promised and left so she could tend to her next appointment.

I rushed to the car and waited for it to warm up. I wanted to go back and see Ken, but I would just wait until tomorrow. The session with Dr. Polin made me think more about what he asked earlier, and I was going to do it. I wanted to make amends with his parents and see my babies. This was a big step for me, and I was proud of myself for taking it.

As I was about to pull off, my phone rang and it was Fancy. I bet she was wondering where I was with her car, so I headed back to her house. I didn't want anyone to know I was going to see a psychologist. This was my own little secret that I wanted to keep until I felt like it was the right time to say something. Until then, no one would know.

"Hey, best. What's that?" I quizzed as Fancy was waiting for me with an envelope in her hand. She held it out to me and sighed.

"This, this is the fake results saying Kendrick was the father," she revealed with sad eyes, only because she knew it would make me think of my unborn.

I would have been six months pregnant with another little girl right now. It was sad that she died from the rage of her father. Instead of burying her in a small little box, I asked them to cremate her and got her ashes sent to a jewelry place to store her in a necklace. Fancy saw the idea on Facebook and thought it would be best. She was the one who paid for it and refused to let me pay her back. I couldn't wait until it got here because I was never taking it off.

"Wow. I can't believe I went to this extent," I said while taking it from her. I walked to the kitchen and found a lighter. Standing over the sink, I lit the paper up and watched it burn slowly. There goes that feeling again; the feeling of feeling lighter. It was a good feeling and I knew that feeling free would be amazing. It was going to take time, but I was patient. Great things take time, right?

ROMAN

Saturday night...

We were at Amari's grand reopening, and I loved how the place had come together. Lola and my baby had done their thing, and it showed. The place was packed with family, friends and loved ones; even some new customers. Since Amari and her crew were busy inking people, I was the one going around thanking everyone for coming out to support. I didn't mind; anything for my baby.

"I love it, son. You did a good job picking this place out," Ma complimented as she admired the new tattoo Amari had just finished. It was the baby's due date in Roman numerals. She said no matter what day the baby was born; the due date would always be special. I didn't understand why, but it wasn't my body.

"Thanks, ma. I'm not what brought it to life, though. It's all Amari and Lola. I just provided the place for them."

"That means you played a big part in it. So, are you still going to do it?" she asked with a huge grin.

Tonight was the night I planned on proposing to Amari. What better time to do it than when we do our pregnancy reveal? This was a special night to Amari, and I wanted to go the extra mile to make it that much more magical. I was nervous as fuck, especially to do it in front of everyone, but I had to suck that shit up and get my wife.

"Yes ma'am, but I'm nervous as hell. What if she says no? I'm tellin' you, Ma; her ass embarrasses me, then I'm going to embarrass her, real shit," I stated seriously and she laughed. This wasn't a game. I was damn near laying my life on the line by doing this, and if her little mean ass said no, then it was over with.

"You and I both know she isn't going to say no, so stop talkin' crazy before I slap you upside the head in front of everyone," she threatened while kissing my cheek, then walked away. I went to mix and mingle with a few other guests before going to check on Amari. I had seen her rush to the bathroom, so I was sure Rome had her spilling her guts out again.

"Hey, baby. You good?" I asked as I knocked on the door.

"It's unlocked, Roman," she said before she started puking again. I opened the door and locked it behind me. I rubbed her back and held her hair as she wiped her mouth with a cool towel.

"I told you to wear your hair up, ma. You always get sick around this time of night. I knew this would happen."

"I... I know. I should have listened," she sighed as she flushed the toilet and I helped her to her feet. She pulled her hair up as I retrieved the toothbrush and toothpaste from her bag and got it prepared for her. "Thank you, baby."

"You know I got you. So, when do you want to make the big announcement? I can't lie, I'm getting anxious."

"When Jersey and my parents get here. I don't want them to miss it. Where's Sincere?" she asked as she started brushing her teeth.

"He texted and said he was on his way about fifteen minutes ago, so he should be pulling up soon," I told her.

"Do you think things will be awkward with him and Jersey? I know they've been doing the whole co-parenting thing, but that's about it. They need to stop bullshittin' and just be together."

"Hey, that's them. I've told Sin what I think, but that's all I can do. He's a grown ass man and Jersey is a grown ass woman. If they want to go around acting like little ass kids, then that's them. They'll realize sooner or later," I stated with a shrug of my shoulders.

To be real, I wasn't trying to hear the shit with them anymore. Sin was my nigga and always would be, but this situation was getting out of hand to me. He told me about his little one-night stand or whatever you want to call it with Kacey. I told him that just opened up a door of more troubles because now, it was going to be hard for them to stay in that friend zone. He assured me it wouldn't go that far again, but his ass was lying. I was a nigga and if I had a female friend that confessed her love for me and then threw the pussy back on me, then I would get up in that shit any chance I got. Well, the old me would have. I'm a one-woman man now and after tonight, that would be secured with a ring.

"You're right. I just hate seeing them be so stubborn." We walked out, hand in hand, and were greeted by her parents with an additional surprise that caused Amari to break down crying in happiness. "Kendrick!"

It took some work, but we were able to convince Dr. Kennings to let Kendrick be released for a few hours to attend tonight. She was very strict on what he could and couldn't do and when we should have him back. I knew it would mean the world to Amari for him to be here, and he didn't want to miss it. He was going to settle for a FaceTime call, but Julian and I pushed the issue and as a result, he was here. Amari ran over and hugged him tightly. To everyone's surprise, he slowly and carefully lifted his arms and hugged her back.

"You know I couldn't miss this big night," Ken said with a smile.

"I'm so happy you're here," Amari cried. "This is the highlight of my night."

Not too long after, Sincere arrived. I greeted him and we done our handshake that ended with a brotherly hug. We couldn't even have a private conversation because Ma came and took him away to talk. Sin would be mad, but I discussed his situation with Ma and she promised to talk to him. I just didn't think she would do it tonight. I discreetly glanced over to where they were sitting and Sin was grilling the fuck out of me. I gave him a thumbs up and went to check with the DJ about the music.

"You got the song, right?" I asked as he changed the song.

"Yeah. You ready for me to play it now?"

"Nah. I'll let you know when it's time."

"Roman!" I heard a tiny voice and knew it was Jo when I felt his arms wrap around my legs. I turned around and picked him up with a smile tugging at my lips.

"What's up, little man. I like this outfit."

"Thank you. My daddy picked it out for me," he beamed with pride.

"Sin?"

"Uh huh. He said I could caww (call) him that and not Sin anymore. Him here?"

"Yeah, buddy. He's right over there. You see him?" I asked as I pointed him out. He jumped down out my arms and ran full speed over to Sin. I watched as Sin's face lit up and how they interacted with one another. Man, I swear I will be crushed if this baby isn't a boy.

"You ready?" Amari walked behind me and whispered in my ear.

"Only if you are."

"Let's do it."

We made our way to the middle of the floor and I cued for the DJ to pause the music. "Excuse me, everyone! May we have your attention, please?"

Everyone stopped what they were doing, and all eyes were on us. I let Amari speak first and then Lola to thank everyone for coming out and supporting. Like always, Lola had a long, dramatic speech that had everyone in tears from laughing. I can't lie, he was the life of the party with his annoying ass.

"Not only is this a celebration for Amari's new shop, but also for us," I started, and everyone was looking around confused except for Jersey, who wore a goofy grin. Amari must have slipped up and told her, but it was cool.

"Roman and I are happy to announce that in July, we will be expecting ba—"

"Oh my gosh! My babies are having a baby!" Ma and A'Marie squealed simultaneously before Amari could finish her statement, and everyone erupted into cheers. They hugged one another and rushed over to hug us. As Ma hugged me, she slipped the ring into my pocket.

"The time is now, son," she whispered in my ear.

"Yes ma'am," I breathed nervously.

I went to the back to get myself together and say a silent prayer that everything went as planned. I jogged out to my car and got the poster boards I needed. When I made it back inside, I saw that Jersey was already working on her part of the plan so I could finish with what I had to do.

I passed the cards out to our families, then stood off to the side where Amari wouldn't be able to see me. I cued the DJ to play the music and dim the lights. Major's *Why I Love You* softly played through the speaker, and I watched as Jersey led Amari to the center of the room again and took her place. As the song played, each person held up a card that I had drawn on. It went from our first date to our first doctor's visit. It took me a long ass time to draw all that, but the priceless expression on Amari's face made it all worth it.

When it was nearing the end, I came from the shadows and quietly walked up behind her and bent down on one knee, just as Jo held the card up that said, "turn around." She turned around and the room went wild as she covered her mouth with her hands and gazed at me in surprise. The DJ turned the music down so I could begin my speech.

"Amari, I love you and our unborn more than life itself. You complete me and I swear, I don't know where I would be without you. From the moment I laid eyes on your little mean ass, I knew you were the one for me. Despite all the bullshit that came with me, you put up with it and showed me what love is all about. You know I'm not the mushy type, but you bring that side out of me, ma. You got me out here thinking I'm the love guru or something."

"You can say that shit again," Sincere yelled, and everyone

laughed. I gave him the finger and turned my attention back to Amari.

"I love you, and I want to spend the rest of my life with you. Now, can you do me the honor and marry me?" I held my breath as I pulled out the ring and waited for her to answer.

"You know damn well I will!" she screamed and jumped into my arms. Since I was still on one knee, I toppled over with her on top of me. We engaged in a deep kiss that made me almost forget anyone else was in the room. Julian cleared his throat and Amari got off me fast. I stood up and placed the fifteen-carat diamond ring on her finger and kissed her again.

The rest of the night was filled with love, laughter, and joy. Everyone seemed to be the happiest; even Jersey and Sin seemed to be getting along. This night turned out to be better than I expected, and I had to thank my family for helping. People slowly started leaving and eventually, it was just Amari and me.

"So, soon to be Mrs. Smiley, how was your night?" I asked as I picked up a few things and she ate. She had been eating all night and didn't plan on stopping until we went to bed.

"It was the best night of my life, thanks to you." She giggled. "You really went the extra mile, Roman. How were you able to pull this off without me knowing?"

"I'm just good like that," I boasted while dusting my shoulder off. "I just used my time wisely. I would work on things when you were taking a nap or out with Lola getting things for the shop. It was hard, but I did it."

"Thank you so much, baby. I love it," she gushed as she admired her ring.

I swaggered over to her and stood in between her legs. I leaned down and planted soft, sensual kisses in the nape of her neck. She leaned her head back and let out a low, sexy moan that made my dick spring to life.

"You know we have to celebrate, right? We can break in that new futon you got in the back," I suggested and pressed my hard against her. I could feel the heat from her pussy and wanted a taste.

"Not uh," she giggled. "We are not getting busy on my new furniture."

"Well, let me get your ass home then because after that performance, I deserve to be in them guts."

"Why you gotta be so nasty?"

"Nasty is my middle name, girl. You ain't know?" I teased, and she hit me.

"You can wait until we get home, but first; we want some ice cream."

"We? So, you're going to use my baby to your advantage, huh?"

"Yup. I'm the one eating for two; not you."

"I guess we can, with your spoiled ass. Just know that ice cream will be put to *good* use," I stated with a wink. She leaned up and gave me a kiss that sent a shiver down my spine. It was crazy what she was doing to me, but that's why I loved her. No one else could make me feel like this.

"I was thinking... I want us to get married on the day we started dating. That way, we can have two anniversaries in one."

"I can dig it. I like that. It means I only have to buy one gift," I joked and she rolled her eyes. "I'm just playing, ma. I love that idea."

"It's set then. We're already off to a good start at this wedding planning."

"We? I'm not doing shit but making sure my black ass is standing at the altar waiting on you. I've watched too much TV with Ma to know how women turn into bridezillas, and I'm not with the shit. I'll let Jersey, A'Marie, and Ma deal with that."

"Oh, whatever. You have to help with something," she pouted.

"You know I will, ma. I was just playin'. This is *our* wedding, which means we are in this together."

"That's why I love you. You always meet me halfway."

"That's how it's supposed to be. I'm your man, so I'll always meet you halfway or come to you. No in between."

"Bushel and a peck."

"Hug around the neck."

We locked up and got ice cream, then headed home. Amari

thought I was playing about the ice cream. Let's just say it put that ass straight to sleep.

EPILOGUE

SINCERE

*T*hanksgiving Day...

I know it was a holiday, but I had to meet with my lawyer before I went to Ma Dukes' house to eat. He was able to squeeze me in and get the adoption papers drawn up for me. Yup, I was serious as fuck when it came to Jo being my son. I told him he could call me daddy, and he took that shit and ran with it. He said it every chance he got and I was ready to change my name, but it was cool. I knew he was just as happy as I was, so I answered any time he called.

At first, Jay wasn't cool with it because I didn't talk to her about it. I understood and apologized for overstepping my boundaries. After that, I called up my lawyer and told him what I needed. Like always, he came through. Now, it was time to present them to Jay and see what she had to say.

As I was heading to Jay's, my phone rang and it was Kacey. I debated on answering it, but since it was a holiday, I did.

"What's up, Kacey. Happy Thanksgiving."

"Happy Thanksgiving to you too, Sin. What are you doing?"

"Not shit. About to go get my grub on. What you up to?"

"Packing."

"Packing? For what? You going to see some family?" I quizzed.

"No. Actually, I'm moving," she confessed, and I had to pull over to make sure I heard her correctly.

"Moving? When?"

"Today."

"Why am I just now finding out, Kacey? I thought we were better than that," I sighed, not trying to hide my disappointment.

I had noticed that after we had sex, Kacey had distanced herself from me. I was confused because she was the one so concerned about it not ruining our friendship, but she was the one who pulled away. Ro thought it was because she didn't want her feelings to get deeper and that was a good point, so I couldn't be too mad. I just missed my friend.

"I'm sorry, Sin. I know things have been funny between us lately, but I had to pull myself away from you. After we had sex, I felt my feelings shift that I couldn't control them. I fell harder for you and I didn't know how to handle it, knowing that you wanted us to only be friends. Pulling away from you until I got myself together seemed to be the best option, so that's what I did. I never meant to intentionally hurt your feelings. I just wanted to save our friendship," she explained, and I understood.

"I appreciate you doing what was best for us, but you still could have told me. You had me thinkin' you weren't fuckin' with a kid anymore."

"I'm always going to fuck with you, Sin. Not literally, though," she joked, and we shared a laugh.

"Why are you moving?"

"I was offered my dream job of having my own office in New York," she stated proudly, and I could hear the happiness in her tone.

"That's what's up, Kacey! I'm proud of you, girl. I guess I'll have to make special trips to NY to see my friend, right?"

"Only if it's okay with Jersey," she said, and I sighed loudly. "Don't do that, Sin. We're friends, remember? I know you love her and you still hold some animosity toward her, but stop being so gotdamn stubborn and get her back! Be the family that Josiah needs. He's who y'all should think about at the end of the day. I listened to you and now, I'm telling you; go be with her."

For Kacey to be telling me this, I knew it was something I needed and low key wanted to do. Jay and I had been in a good space, and it was bringing back some old feelings. I found myself thinking about her throughout the day and wanted to call or text her, but my pride wouldn't let me. I glanced at the adoption papers in my passenger seat and knew what I had to do. If not us, Jo deserved to be happy with both his parents; even if we weren't blood. We were all he knew, and that's how it would remain.

"I guess you're right," I sighed. "You sure you're not feeling any type of way by telling me this?"

"No, I'm good because I want my friend to be happy, and she's your happiness. Why wouldn't I want better for you?"

"I'm going to miss you, Kacey."

"And I'm going to miss you more. Thank you for coming back into my life. Promise not to leave again?"

"I promise."

"Thank you. Now, go get you woman back and let me finish packing. My flight leaves in a few hours and I want to get some rest before I go."

"Call me before you leave, okay?"

"I will. Be safe, Sin."

We ended the call and I had to just sit there to gather my thoughts for a minute. All along, I knew the reason behind why I didn't want to be with Kacey in that way, but it took her to tell me for me to truly accept it. Jay was who my heart was with, and it was time I let her know.

I hopped back on the road with a new attitude. For the first time in a while, I was happy. The only person who could bring out that emotion was Jo for a while; up until now. I stopped at the store up the street from Jay's house to get her some flowers and a toy for Jo. He would be mad if I came with something for his mama and not him.

I made it in her driveway and killed the engine. I grabbed everything I needed and jogged up the front steps. I knocked on the door with a smile on my face and waited for her to answer. Minutes went by as I knocked and rang the doorbell to never get an answer. I pulled my phone out to call her and was sent straight to voicemail. Immediately, the worst-case scenarios bombarded my brain, so I kicked the door down and ran inside to find it empty.

What in the fuck is going on here?

I searched the house and noticed that some of their things were gone. That was weird. I tried calling Jay again and got mad when I got the box. I was about to go out and look for them when a note laying on the table beside the door caught my eyes. I walked over and felt the tears cascade down my face as I read what Jay had wrote.

Dear Sincere,

I knew you would come here today to find us gone, but I want to explain. First, I want to say that I'm sorry I didn't tell you, but it's easier this way. If I would have told you we were leaving, you would have flipped out, and I wanted to avoid that encounter. It was hard for me to make this decision; the decision to take Jo from you and move back home. The decision to quit my job and keep this from Amari as well. It was a selfish choice, I know. Just know this move is only temporary and we will be back in a few months— hopefully.

The reason we had to up and leave is because Mama needed my help. Her husband, Don, has stage three lung cancer and she needed me to be there for her. I couldn't just leave her hanging. What type of daughter would I be? She's my mother, and I know she would drop everything to be here for me if it came to that again.

There's something else that I want you to know. I love you, Sincere. I hate that things happened the way they did between us and like I've said before, I would go back and change things if I could. While I was in that cold, dreary basement that bitch had me locked up in, it gave me time to think about everything. At first, I thought it all was just a sign that we shouldn't be together and the choice we made was for the best. But, when I called that day we escaped and you answered, I knew you would always be here for us. You didn't save us once, but twice. You went out your way to make sure we were fine. You could have gotten killed, but you risked it all to help us, and I can never repay you for that.

You moving on with her has hurt me more than you can imagine. I scold myself every day for not being the woman you deserved; for not being the woman you wanted me to be. I just thank you for not letting that affect the relationship and bond you have with Josiah. That little boy adores you and the ground you walk on. He's more hurt than I am about leaving because he didn't get to say bye or give you a hug. I feel like a bad parent for him being so upset, but he doesn't understand the place we are in now and why I chose to do so.

So, I came up with my own conclusion. Underneath this note is an extra plane ticket, for you. Come with us. I still love you, Sincere, and I know the feeling is mutual. I'm not trying to ruin your new relationship, I just need to know that you still want this as bad as I do; that you want us as your family. If you show up, then we can take this one day at a time and work on rebuilding what we started, but even better. If you don't, then I understand and I will only contact you if it has something to do with Josiah. The ball is in your court, Sincere, and I pray that you pass it to me. I'll be waiting.

XOXO,

Jay

To Be Continued...

Please, continue reading...

NOTE FROM THE AUTHOR:

Hey, guys! First, I want to say thank you all so much for rocking with me and taking time out to read my craft! I hope you all enjoy it just as much as I do writing.

Now, I know some of you were probably shocked to see that TBC above, but let me explain.

I have really and truly fell in love with these characters and what they have going on in life. They hold a special place in my heart.

Doing a part four was something I went back and forth with myself constantly as I was writing this book. My first thought was what would the readers think? Will it be too much? But, as I continued writing, more thing came to mind and decided to take a shot and do part four.

I want to show the growth of these characters and how their story ends. I want to show the adoption process of Josiah and the pregnancy and wedding planning for Amari and Roman. I didn't want to short you all of anything. It's so much more to these characters that I want to give and that's exactly what I'm going to do. Trust me, book four will be the last one! I hope you all understand and continue rocking with me. Part four will be coming in September; I promise not to keep you all waiting long! Thank you and oh, please don't forget to leave a review!

Note from the author:

With love,
DeeAnn

ALSO BY DEEANN

If You Stay Down, I'll Stay True 2
By Tricee
Part One is #Free

Grab This Completed Series,
Part One is #Free

Read All Three Parts Now!

Read All Three Parts Now!

CPSIA information can be obtained
at www.ICGtesting.com
Printed in the USA
LVHW05s0337171018
593814LV00021B/243/P